Clare Connell
over fifty ror
including novels in the Harlequin ...
Modern and Dare series.

For sneak-peeks at new-releases, covers, and to win
exclusive members-only content, sign up to the CC
newsletter, or follow Clare on facebook.

To apply to become a CC Advance Reader, and get your
hands on e-books ahead of publication in exchange for an
honest review, please email clare@clareconnelly.co.uk

You can also follow Clare on Amazon and BookBub to get
alerts for new releases.

Happy reading!

First published 2019

(c) Clare Connelly

Cover Credit: adobestock

Contact Clare:

http://www.clareconnelly.com

Blog: http://clarewriteslove.wordpress.com/

Email: Clare@ClareConnelly.co.uk

Follow Clare Connelly on facebook for all the latest.

Join Clare's Newsletter to stay up to date on all the latest CC news. www.clareconnelly.com

❀ Created with Vellum

THE SHEIKH'S INHERITED BRIDE

PROLOGUE

H E'D DIED WHILE SHE was somewhere over the Atlantic, probably catching up on old episodes of Friends. He'd died while she was high in the sky, and she'd wondered if his spirit had passed through the aircraft, on its way to heaven.

She hadn't known, until she'd landed in Abu Faya. Nothing had seemed amiss, at first, but once the plane had touched down and the aircraft doors had opened, the country's chief security minister had met her, his expression somber.

"*Sharafaha*," he addressed her with the deference due her position, as someone who was the consort to the King of this country. "We must leave, quickly."

She was impatient to be back in the palace now. She'd been in America with Bella for two weeks, and as much as she loved her sister, and adored spending time with her, Sophia had no doubts her real life was here in Abu Faya. Her future, too. Her blonde hair, long and loose, carried in the sultry desert air, lifting off her face, and she caught it in one hand, the diamond ring on her finger glinting in the afternoon sunlight.

"Why? Has something happened?"

He met her eyes and then looked away once more. "Now, *Sharafaha.*"

Displeasure at having not been answered sat inside of her, but she ignored it, suppressing her irritation as she had learned to do over the years. Sheikhas did not roll their eyes, nor sigh audibly. Sheikhas did not express what they might be feeling, even when they were feeling it in every bone of their body.

Settled in the back of the limousine, she lifted her phone from her bag and tried calling Addan. It rung out. She texted him instead, "Just landed. What's going on?"

She put the phone away, her eyes chasing the sights of this country she loved so much as the limousine ate up the miles. The airport was nestled in desert, just a few low-lying buildings surrounded it, but beyond the desert was the enormous, modern city of Khatra, a place of wealth, privilege and dreams. It had been forged from the ideas of mankind, and it stood now as a sentinel to their strength and formidable spirit when their attention was properly focused. Khatra was a city that survived in the face of extreme adversity – it had grown from nothing and stood proud.

It was a city for dreamers, a city for doers, and beyond its magnificent modernity was the ancient, sand-swept landscape the country was famed for. Deserts, dunes, oases and the Bedouin tribes that moved around, seeking one another out, following the historic customs of this place.

It was a twenty minute drive from the airport to the palace. She watched the undulations of the land and finally, the palace rose as if by magic from the sands that had created it. She would never grow tired of that sight. As they

approached, she remembered the first time she'd seen it –
then as a small child who believed in fairytales and magic,
who thought princes were the creation of Hans Christian
Andersen and desert principalities the providence of the
Arabian nights stories her father had loved to read her. All
white walls and curling turrets, windows carved like teardrops
into the sides, and palm trees lining the entrance and forming
a perimeter. There were roses too, and persimmons, quinces
and pomegranates forming an edible but impenetrable hedge.
As children, she and Addan had built houses from the thickets,
and when she'd pricked her finger on the thorn of a pomegranate bush, he'd wiped the blood away with his white shirt
and kissed her fingertip better. She'd been eight and he'd been
twelve – but they'd become best friends that day. Brother and
sister before they'd had any thought of marriage.

The car pulled to a stop at the entrance to the palace; she
didn't notice anything except the fragrance of the night-
flowering jasmine that was beginning to sweeten the air,
taking away the day's sultry heat, replacing it with romance
and beauty.

"Where is Addan, Minister Hereth?" She asked, moving
towards the large doors that led to the palace.

"This way," he kept his head bowed low and moved
quickly, preceding her into the marble corridor. Ancient
tapestries ran along its length, each telling a story of the
country's heritage. As a child, she'd spent days learning about
them and trying to draw them. Once, she'd reached out to
touch one, to feel the nobbled stitches in the time-worn
fabric, but Addan had grabbed her fingers and held them,
shaking his head.

"It's back luck," he'd said, in that way he had, that made it
impossible to know if he was joking or not.

"I don't believe in bad luck," she had responded defiantly,

her sharp chin tilted in an angle of defiance, her blue eyes firing dismissively.

Six months later her father had died, and she'd learned that there was such a thing as loss and luck and curses and fate – the very bottom had dropped out of her world, wrenching her violently from everything she knew.

Only Addan had been there, dear Addan, looking into her eyes comfortingly, his own young face stretched by an empathy she hadn't then understood. *"I know this feeling, Sophia; I've held it in my heart, just like you. Disbelief and rage, despair at your powerlessness. I wish I could take it away for you, but I can't. I can hold your hand though, and promise you this will get better."* And he'd smiled, extending his palm and she'd felt a glimmer of hope that everything really would be okay, one day.

Minister Hereth led Sophia through the corridors of the palace, corridors she knew as well as she'd ever known at any home in her life. At the door to Addan's office, Hereth came to a stop and knocked on its shining wooden surface, his skin unusually pale.

Sophia studied the taut lines of his face, in profile, and her heart rate kicked up a notch. "Minister, is something the matter?"

He didn't answer at first and then, as the door opened inwards, "Yes, *Sharafaha*. There is."

She blinked at him. "What? What's happened?"

He didn't speak. Her nerves stretched taut. Warily, she stepped inside.

"Addan?" She shook her hair loose from the pale head-scarf she wore, draping it over the back of a chair. "Whatever is going on?"

But the dark figure by the window was not that of the man she was going to marry. Where Addan had been tall yet slim, elegant in his build, his brother Malik was a warrior, cast from the same tribal mold of Kings who had ruled this country for eons.

It was Malik who turned slowly to face her; Malik whose eyes, so black they were like shining coal, regarded her with the coldness and guardedness that had always been a part of his response to her – as though he instinctively didn't like nor trust her.

And heat flicked at her spine, the instant, unwelcome recognition a biological response to him she had learned to flatten, to ignore. A response she was glad she didn't have to fight often – by silent yet mutual consent, they avoided one another as much as possible.

She hadn't seen Malik in months, since he'd come to Addan's birthday ball with a Swedish supermodel, and danced with the stunning woman all night, his body cleaved to hers, his eyes promising seduction and heat that had made Sophia blush. And she'd stared at them. She'd stared at his body, the way he flicked his hips and the woman's eyes had swept shut. They'd danced but it had been so intimate, so sexy, and something like a raging fire of lust had burst in her gut.

She blushed now at the memory, and to cover it, assumed an expression of cross impatience. "What are you doing here?" She forgot, in that moment, that she generally attempted to preserve an air of respect. He was, after all, second in line to the throne. Besides which, Addan adored him – and revered him in equal measure.

"There was an accident, earlier today."

Her brows lifted, as she waited for him to continue.

The thick column of his neck, covered in dark stubble, shifted, as he seemed to weigh what he was going to say next. "My brother died."

The words, spoken in her native English, jarred, like stones in the sole of her shoe. She heard them but she couldn't make sense of what he'd said, she couldn't unravel his statement. She shook her head, certain he'd misspoken or she'd misunderstood.

"I'm sorry," she lifted a hand to her throat, toying with the necklace there – a gift from Addan a long time ago. "What did you say?"

"Addan is dead."

Belatedly, realization hit Sophia and she stumbled backwards, reaching for something – anything – to support her. Only there was nothing, just air, and it was not thick enough to provide any kind of strength. She shook her head, unable to accept this, needing him to explain why he would say something so cruel, why he would lie to her.

But mistaking her anger for something weaker, he crossed the room and gripped her shoulders, holding her steady when she might otherwise have fallen. He stared down at her with the sense of resentment that was familiar to Sophia. "It was an accident." The words were steely, but she heard the condemnation beneath the surface. "It happened quickly."

Grief splintered through her, tearing her apart. "I don't believe it."

"I understand." His lips were grim. "Nor did I, at first."

"It can't be…"

"I have seen his body," he said, and she realized she was being held by the only person on earth who could understand the emptiness of her heart. That Addan's death bonded them in an awful, horrifying way.

"I'm so sorry," she said, looking up at him, seeing the pain, the raw despair in his stony features and sobbing suddenly. "What happened?" She asked again.

"The helicopter he was flying; the blades stalled."

"Don't," she shuddered, burying her face in Malik's shirt, his masculine, musky fragrance lacing through her on a biological level. "Don't tell me he took that damned thing…"

Addan had been restoring an old helicopter for years, tinkering with it, loving it for its rudimentary nature.

"It doesn't matter now. Don't you understand?" A muscle throbbed, low in his jaw, and he guided her to Addan's desk chair, placing her down on it. But she didn't want to sit there. She didn't want to sit *at all*, but especially not where Addan had been so at home. She jerked out of the chair, her body still weak from shock, her mind slow and groggy. "He's gone. He's gone."

She sobbed, lifting her hands to her lips, the words so cold, so violent for their truth, and the reality they painted.

"I'm so sorry," she said again.

"As am I."

Her eyes shifted to Malik's face as the full reality of this situation wrapped around her. "You are King," she said, sitting into Addan's chair now, collapsing into it, taking in a shaking breath.

"Yes," he crossed his arms over his chest, "I will inherit Addan's throne, and all that entails."

She swallowed, his promotion one she knew he didn't wish for, one she knew he didn't take any joy in. Addan had said, many times, that Malik – eleven months younger – should have been born first. That he was the natural born leader. And while Sophia could see that Malik had the strength to be Sheikh, it was also abundantly clear he had zero desire for the role.

Sheikh Malik bin Hazari was a renowned playboy prince. Never at the palace, always off sleeping his way around Europe.

How many times had she opened a news website on her phone to see his photo? At a fashion parade, on a celebrity's yacht, a glamorous beach, always with a beautiful woman at his side. Something heated sparked inside of her. Sympathy, she told herself, because that life of his was at an end.

He can do that, Sharafaha, because he is not the heir, Addan had pointed out, when she'd questioned him once over Malik's antics.

And yet, his destiny was now to lead, to take up Addan's role within this ancient Kingdom. Everything would change. Addan's death shifted the whole world – or Sophia's part of it, at least.

"Your highness," she spoke softly, the words almost impossible to catch. "I'd like to be alone now."

He didn't answer, his eyes holding hers for a moment before she spun and moved to the door. But as her fingers curved around the handle, poised to open it, his voice arrested her.

"You are part of that, *Sharafaha.*"

She turned to face him. "Part of what?"

"When he died, I inherited all that was his. Including you."

A *frisson* of alarm jolted her spine. "I don't... understand."

"This palace, the title, the country, his duties. All of it. And also, your betrothal to Addan, on his death, by unbreakable law, passed to me."

CHAPTER 1

"YOU ARE SHAKING." Malik's lips compressed with impatience and Sophia shifted her gaze towards him, wishing he weren't right. Wishing, with all her heart, she could get control of nerves that were firing through her body like sparks of electricity.

She couldn't, and she was far too proud to deny the obvious. And so she tilted her chin defiantly, shooting him what she hoped passed for a withering look. "I'm aware of that."

Her honesty didn't, apparently, earn her any bonus points with the man she was hours away from marrying.

"You are afraid of me?"

He stood six and a half feet tall, muscle and sinew, a warrior in a King's clothes, a warrior with a heart of steel. Yes. She was afraid; she was terrified. Years ago – as a teenager, she had agreed to marry her best friend; she had thought she'd be walking down the aisle towards the kind-hearted King Addan, who adored her, who had wrapped a bandage around her knee when she was only eight years old, and she'd run through a hedge of pomegranate, scratching herself all over.

"Do you think I mean to hurt you?" He crossed his arms over his chest, glaring down his nose at her, his symmetrical features covered in a sprinkling of facial hair incredibly distracting.

"No," she heard herself say, shaking her head from side to side, then pressing her fingers against her stomach. The lace of the traditional, royal Abu Fayan bridal outfit was rough under her fingertips. It didn't matter, anyway. No matter how she pressed, the butterflies wouldn't go away. "It's just... not what I'd expected."

She tried to smile, but her features were too tense.

His eyes, blacker than the night sky, widened, and his brow furrowed. "This is not what *either* of us expected," he agreed. He had long, dark hair, and he wore it pulled into a somewhat messy bun on top of his head. Addan had been neat. Trim. Well-groomed. The opposite to his brother.

A shiver ran down her spine as again she saw her intended groom as some kind of wild creature, feral and free-roaming, dragged in from the desert, barely contained by this exquisitely beautiful palace.

"You know how the wedding ceremony will go?"

She swallowed, closing her eyes as she tried to push the details from her mind. But she couldn't. They were there, as she'd understood them for years. And again, when she'd been going to marry Addan, nothing had worried her; she'd welcomed every intimacy.

Standing opposite *this* man though, singing to him in his native language, reciting the ancient poetry of the Bedouins who'd first inhabited this prosperous land, she felt like a part of her was going to be stripped raw for him to see.

"Yes," she nodded, concealing her fear with care.

"And you know what comes afterwards?" His nostrils

flared with the challenge, as he studied her with deep concentration.

The tradition was one she and Addan had laughed about, like school children planning to fool their parents and stay up until midnight for the first time. The idea of a couple being locked in a tower for twenty four hours to consummate their marriage had seemed silly, but for a culture that saw its regal bloodline as its most valuable asset, it was one they'd been prepared to honour.

Now? Being locked in a tower with Sheikh Malik bin Hazari? Her nerve endings jangled inside of her, and her stomach was in knots. She'd hinted to her valet that perhaps it wasn't necessary in the twenty first century – the very idea it could be dispensed with was met with incredulity.

The tower was happening.

"Yes," she dropped her gaze, unable to look at him.

But he closed the distance between them and lifted her face to his, holding her chin between his thumb and forefinger, forcing her gaze to lock to his. "You are apprehensive about sleeping with me?"

Heat suffused her cheeks, his directness completely unexpected. "I'm..." she bit down on her lower lip, then stopped when his eyes chased the movement and she felt the whip of electricity slash her spine. "We hardly know one another." She shrugged her slender shoulders.

"And you knew my brother," he said, the words blanked of any emotion.

"He was my best friend," she whispered, and tears thickened in her throat. She blinked her eyes furiously, not willing to destroy the make up artist's work nor to show any hint of weakness to this man.

Her groom was quiet a moment, his jaw clenched, a muscle throbbing at its base.

"We do not need to know one another." His gaze moved

over her face. "This is a political marriage, a treaty of sorts. You will have your duties, and outside of them, your own life. You will carry on much as you did before."

Her heart stammered inside her chest. "Except for the whole having sex together thing?" She pushed, her eyes holding his, a silent challenge in them.

His expression shifted to one of distaste. "Yes."

Great. He was as reluctant to go to bed with her as she was with him. Only Sophia knew that deep down, her reluctance had a more troubling root, that there was far more to her hesitation.

Hadn't she always found him compelling? Hadn't she found one look from him could make her knees tremble? Her pulse race? Her reaction to him had terrified her, so she'd done her best to stay away from him, avoiding him assiduously whenever he was due to be at the palace. "It's nice for you and your brother to have time together," she'd teased Addan, when he'd tried to include her in their lunches. "Besides, I have reading to do."

"Always reading," Addan had teased back, kissing the tip of her nose before turning back to Malik, who had been watching the interaction with that same look of steely disapproval on his features he always held.

"With Addan's death, the need for an heir became more pressing. We cannot afford to wait. I am the end of this family's line – we must have a child, and fast."

Her stomach looped in on itself. "I know that." It was a whisper. A soft plea.

"You hate the idea of it, don't you?" he asked, grimly, his eyes sweeping over her. "You hate the idea of sleeping with the brother of the man you loved?"

Her eyes fell closed, her heart stuttering.

She *had* loved Addan. She had loved him, depended on him, adored him. Not in a romantic way, though. Theirs had been a friendship, first and foremost – deeper than any she'd ever known.

She didn't have a chance to answer – there was a knock on the door a moment later and Malik straightened, taking a step back from her. "Come," he spoke in English for her benefit, despite the fact she'd been fluent in Abu Fayan for years.

A servant entered, bowing low. "Majesty, *Sharafaha*, it is time."

"One minute," Malik dismissed, turning back to face Sophia.

"You were engaged to Addan," he said, when the door was closed once more, leaving them in privacy. "And though I am about to pledge myself to you, to declare myself your husband, and you my wife, let us both say, in this room, that I will always consider you his." His eyes bore into hers, hot and yet somehow making her cold all over.

"We will have sex tonight, but it will never be the love making you and he enjoyed." He expelled harshly, his expression showing true disgust. "I regret the necessity of this. If only you and he had been married, we would never have been forced into this marriage." He turned his back on her, looking towards the windows. "The idea of taking you from him, even now in death…"

The words were strange, discordant, and her heart ached. She'd been so focused on her own grief and adjustments that she hadn't even thought about how this must have been for Malik. And though she hardly knew him, she was a compassionate and empathetic person, and she moved towards him, coming to stand in front of him, more conscious than usual of the difference in their size.

"We didn't…"

He jerked his head towards her.

"We never slept together," she said quietly, dropping her

gaze and missing the way Malik's expression shifted, tightened, darkened. "Our relationship wasn't... I loved him very much, Malik, but we hadn't... been physically intimate."

A hiss escaped from between his teeth and he gripped her face with both hands, staring at her as though he'd never seen her before. "I don't believe you."

She frowned. "Why would I lie?"

"I cannot say. But I saw you together. I heard the way he spoke about you. You and he were an item for years." The words were imbued with harsh anger. "There is no way you had not been to bed..."

She sighed quietly. "We were getting married. We knew that from a young age. It seemed right to wait..."

He swore in his own tongue, and then a harsh laugh escaped him, humourless, laced with pain. "So he was denied even this?" He shook his head angrily, and took a step away from her and his whole body was tight with feelings and they were echoing inside of her. He spun around to face her. "You are a virgin."

It was a statement, so she didn't answer.

"This," he spoke slowly, enunciating the word carefully, "is not how it is supposed to be."

———

THE TOWER WAS BEAUTIFUL. An ancient section of the palace carved from marble, it stood high above the earth like a beacon, an ancient monolith, reaching for the azure sky. There were no lifts. Hundreds of steps – carved from stone – led to the top, with a dip in the centre of each, from centuries of use. And at the very pinnacle of the tower, an enormous room, sparsely furnished, except for an enormous bed at its centre.

A carved, timber door led to a bathroom, with a large

bath – almost like a small swimming pool – a shower big enough to accommodate two, and all the amenities.

"There are clothes in there, for you," his voice came from across the room. She turned, almost guiltily, to see him watching her. He'd removed his ceremonial robe, leaving him in just loose white pants.

His bare chest wanted to drag her eyes downwards but she resisted the temptation, even when her mouth went dry and her pulse shot into overdrive.

"So we're locked in here for how long?" She asked, though she knew.

"When darkness falls, tomorrow, a bell will toll, and we will be released," he muttered, and she would have laughed for how absurd all of this was – for how little pleasure her husband obviously took in the idea of going to bed with his wife.

And she understood – he didn't want her. She'd seen the women he ordinarily dated. Women who were glamorous and exotic, incredibly sophisticated. Sophia was nothing like that, nothing like them.

Neither of them had chosen this, but here they were: husband and wife.

"I suppose we should just get it over with then?"

At this, she had the feeling he was holding back a laugh. "Do you now?"

"We have to sleep together; I get it. You need a little Sheikh or Sheikha to groom in your own image. And I married you knowing that. So?"

Another laugh. "My young, innocent wife," he murmured, prowling across the tiled floor, shaking his head. "I thought you were concerned by the fact we aren't acquainted?" He stood so close she could feel the heat of his body and breathe in his woody, alpine scent. So close her knees were shaking and she had to push aside the horrible wave of guilt towards

Addan. She wished she could summon more resistance, more cool disdain, for what was about to happen. She wished her pulse wasn't a firestorm within her soul.

Contradictory feelings scored deep into her heart.

But she had married Malik, and she knew Addan would have wanted this. Duty had bound him, deepest of all; his country had been his true love. He would be pleased she was using what she knew of Abu Faya and her training for this position. She'd been raised to be Sheikha, and she was simply fulfilling her destiny.

In a strange, uneasy world, Addan would have wanted this.

"We don't need to know one another," she pointed out, lifting a hand up to the wedding outfit. The henna ink was all over the backs of her hands, leaving intricate patterns that had captivated her as the illustrations had been rendered.

"True," he said, watching as she pushed the sleeves down. But before she could slide it over her breasts, he shook his head.

"Let me."

Her tummy knotted. "Why?"

"A groom should have the honour of undressing his bride," he said, simply, moving behind her and standing so close his powerful thighs brushed the backs of her legs and bottom. His hands came to her bare shoulders, and she sucked in a large gulp of air as he ran his fingers over her flesh, exploring, investigating, familiarizing himself.

She bit down on her lower lip, aware a groan was making its way from the pit of her stomach to the tip of her tongue, and wanting to contain it as long as possible. He ran his hands lower, to the tops of her arms, before connecting with the lace of the fabric and sliding it lower and lower, slowly, so, so, slowly, so the dress shifted downwards, over her breasts and back, revealing her to the room, if not to him.

And she was grateful he was behind her, so she could take a moment to get used to this, to brace for the fact he was going to see her *naked*.

He moved his hands to her waist, holding the dress there, leaving it, as his fingers feathered over her skin, brushing the smooth, creamy flesh. She held her breath as his fingers crept upwards slowly – so slowly – until they brushed the underside of her breasts and she could no longer stave off the groan. It escaped low and hungry. His head dropped lower, his breath fanning the sensitive flesh at the side of her neck as his hands lifted higher, brushing over her breasts so lightly she pushed forward, needing more.

She thought she heard him laugh, but perhaps she'd imagined it, because when she leaned back, pressing against him, surrendering to what he was doing to her completely, she felt his rock hard body behind her – all of him, so hard, so incredibly hard that her cheeks flushed pink. And now his hands weren't slow, nor gentle. They cupped her breasts, feeling their weight in his hands and he spoke to her, low and soft, in words that were familiar yet not, words that were close to Abu Fayan but must have been a dialect for she didn't know them; words that sounded magical and breathed magic all around her.

When his fingers curled around her nipples, squeezing them, she let out a cry of surprise, hoarse and low at the same time, and then her body was writhing and she wanted more of this, more of him plucking at her nipples, pulling at their sensitive tips, flicking them with his insistent fingers. She pushed her body backwards and one hand dropped lower, to the dress, and inside it, gliding down her flat stomach to the flimsy lace thong she'd been dressed in that morning.

Per Abu Fayan traditions, she'd been waxed bare, and his fingers glided over the flesh of her womanhood, parting her seam as his other hand continued to torment her nipple. He brushed her sex until he found the sensitive cluster of nerves at her clitoris and he moved faster, and now his tongue lashed her neck and she whimpered, her body quivering and shaking for a completely different reason.

Pleasure built inside of her like some kind of wave; a wave she'd never before surfed and yet it had no care for her lack of experience, it was grabbing her and dragging her along the surface, so she couldn't breathe, couldn't speak. She tilted her head back and now his teeth clipped the skin at her neck, just enough to make her cry out and then he was sucking, while his fingers plucked her nipple again and again and his hand drove her higher and higher and she was – in that moment – incoherent, and completely *his*, just as she'd vowed in the ceremony.

"Look at yourself," he muttered, turning her slightly, angling her so she could see their reflection in the mirror, placed in the corner of the room.

Her instinct was to look away, but he growled. "Watch yourself come, watch what your husband can do to you."

And then, she couldn't look away, she was mesmerized, as his dark head dipped forward and he chose another place on her shoulder and began to suck and she saw he'd marked her flesh, marked her with a pale, pink circle from his ministrations, and he was doing so again, and a rush of pleasure fired inside of her at this – at being marked. It wasn't worthy of her and in a calmer moment, she might push the idea away but in this mad slice of time, high in a tower above Abu Faya, she felt it all.

She felt the depravity of having sex with someone she didn't know, of having married a stranger. Worse, a man she actively despised! And she gave herself over to it.

He moved his hand lower, then drove a finger inside of her and she bucked backwards as stars filled her eyes at this unfamiliar invasion. He lifted his head, his eyes meeting hers in the mirror, and he spoke low and huskily in the strange, ancient dialect and with a finger inside of her and his hand moving over her breasts, he held her tight, he watched her, as her very first orgasm drew her onto the top of the wave and tumbled her deep, deep under the surface...

HER INNOCENCE WAS STARTLINGLY OBVIOUS, even if he hadn't known as many women as he had. The way she trembled and shook, the wide-eyed look of surprise as her orgasm wrapped around her, he felt her inexperience in every single minute change of expression, every husky exhalation, every movement.

He stared at her, his eyes devouring her reflection as wave after wave of pleasure had her face crumpled and her body vibrating in his arms.

Malik loved sex.

He'd loved it for as long as he could remember.

And because he'd never had the pressure of carrying on the royal lineage, he'd been happy – and free – to sleep with whomever he wanted. Addan had turned a blind eye to his younger brother's ways, even when Malik knew how little Addan approved.

Malik loved sex. But sleeping with this woman, the woman his brother had loved?

It tore through him, he was sickened by the very idea – worse, he was sickened by how much he wanted her.

Sex is just sex, he told himself, staring at her pale, near-naked body – so American, so different to his caramel complexion, skin that had been ordained for this desert country's climate.

This woman was like satin and moonlight, the petal of a fragile, cream-coloured rose. Her hair was the colour of the beaches of Tharani, all gold and glossy with silver strands flecked through. Her nipples were pale pink, so sweet, giving new meaning to the idea of strawberries and cream. They were hard too, begging for his touch. Her body was covered in goose bumps. He stared down at her, telling himself she was Addan's, she would always be Addan's, except in this one way.

Her body had to be his.

It was unavoidable.

This was just sex.

He'd had enough meaningless sex to be able to add this – to add her – to the catalogue. Addan had never slept with her – no one had. They were married, and within moments, he would possess her completely.

He could absolve himself of any guilt here, and yet he didn't. Guilt was there, possessing him, controlling him, tormenting him. She was Addan's.

Sophia's lips parted and her body shifted, the shock-waves of her first orgasm making her moan a little.

There was nothing for it – they would sleep together until she was pregnant and then he would go back to pretending he could ignore her.

CHAPTER 2

H E HATED HIMSELF, BUT he pushed that aside, telling himself he needed to do this, telling himself they both knew why this was important. He watched as slowly, her breathing returned to normal, as the muscles spasming around his finger calmed; he watched as her eyes went from the fevered wildness of a moment ago to a look of confusion, and then the dawning of embarrassment, and he refused to let her feel that.

"You are my wife," he growled, as much for his own benefit as hers. "This is natural. Normal. Expected."

The fine column of her throat shifted as she swallowed convulsively and he pulled his hands from her body, just for a moment, just so he could move his grip to her hips, where the fine, lace dress sat firm. He held her gaze in the mirror, challenging her to look away before he pushed the dress lower, over the swell of her neat buttocks, and down her legs. He crouched, then, and pressed a kiss to the curve of one perfect butt cheek. She pushed her head back, and he heard his name in her throat, like it was trapped there, and his body tensed.

This should have been Addan. She should have been Addan's.

He flattened his mouth, reminding himself this was just sex, that she was just a woman who'd been trained for the role of his bride, and that included this.

He guided the dress to her ankles until she stepped out of it and then he stood, swiftly, and lifted her, carrying her to the bed; there was no sense in prolonging this, in taking his time with the seduction.

He'd get her out of his system, that was all he needed to do. To get this over with so he could begin moving on. She was his wife, and sex was going to be a part of their relationship. It was a simple transaction; it wasn't a betrayal of Addan.

He stared down at her naked body, her beautiful naked body, her face flushed with pleasure, pupils huge, lips parted, and his gut churned, because he was enjoying this so much more than he should.

"My country needs an heir," he said, simply, pushing his pants down.

Her eyes dragged down his body and he watched her, looking at him, and her cheeks blushed more, and her lips closed, as she stared at his erect cock and he hated that he was going to be her first, even when he loved that he was.

"I am sorry," he heard himself say, as his hands moved back to her supple skin, parting her legs, and he moved his body over her.

"What for?" She asked quietly, her American accent thicker now than usual.

"If it weren't for the necessity of a child, this could be... left. We would not have to rush..."

At that, her eyes flared wide. "I don't think I see any point in delaying the inevitable. Do you?"

His expression hardened. "No."

And so, they were back to how this had all began, with her bare challenge to get this over. To just do it.

He ground his teeth, looking at her face, watching her, wondering at her lack of fear, when before their wedding she'd been quivering all over.

"You will tell me if it hurts," he said, with uncharacteristic gentleness.

"You'd better believe it."

He bit back a laugh, his hands finding her thighs and spreading them wider, and the tip of his cock nudged at her womanhood. She grabbed her breath in her lungs and held it there.

He told himself to be gentle. He told himself to go slowly, to savour this, but his body was fighting him, desperate to take her, desperate to drive his hard length into her sweet core, to rid her of her innocence, to meld his body to hers. He was desperate for her in a way that disgusted him, and angered him.

"Don't prolong," she said, anxious now, and he saw in her eyes the fear at what was about to happen. His disgust grew. His disgust at this arrangement, at the marriage that was necessitated by his country's political needs, at his brother's death, at his brother's betrothal, and at this woman. This innocent foreigner who was to carry in her body the heir to his country. Plenty of women had begged him to sleep with them, had cried out his name, screamed it into the air, their voices husky with passion, sometimes, two women at once, fawning over his body, driving him wild as he prepared to return that favour.

None had looked at him with a sense of reluctant anger, a stoic determination, and told him to get on with it.

He expelled a breath. He was overthinking this. It was Addan.

The fact his brother had loved her, and lost her – and all he deserved in life.

A year had passed – the respectful period of mourning had been observed.

He braced his arms on either side of her head, his powerful body above hers, and stared down into her beautiful face. Eyes that seemed to show everything she felt, that had seemed to sparkle with acerbic amusement when she teased Addan were now laced with pride and determination.

It rankled.

"Just do it," she demanded, lifting her hips up, and he heard what she didn't say. *Get it over with.*

Male pride and ego flared in his gut.

No woman had ever treated his love-making with such clear contempt, and suddenly, he was fired by a desire to exceed every expectation she had, to show her just what it felt like to lose her mind to sex.

He could offer her nothing else – no love, no companionship, no comparison to what she and Addan had known.

But he could give her pleasure. He dropped his head to hers, his mouth so close to hers he felt her warm breath snatching from her.

"I'm going to make you scream my name, *sharafaha*," he ground out, tipping his cock over her seam. She moaned softly, her eyes still flecked with anxiety. "Again," he nudged her thighs further apart. "And again," he pushed his arousal deeper, and her moan grew louder. "And again."

Then, he thrust into her hard and fast, kissing her mouth, swallowing her little gasp of surprise at his possession, absorbing her cry, tasting the brief shock of pain, waiting for it to pass before he pulled out of her and drove himself back in.

She was very still beneath him, her small, fragile body

completely unused to this invasion. "Don't stop." It was a whisper. A hoarse plea that surprised them both.

What surprised him more though was how much he liked hearing her say that. He was ashamed by how much he wanted her to beg him.

"Don't stop, who?" he murmured against her ear, dropping his mouth to her breast, rubbing his stubbled jaw over her sensitive flesh before rolling a delectable nipple in his mouth, his tongue tracing the erect tip, feeling every little dip in her skin, tormenting her with the lightness of his touch. He pulled himself from her, just enough for her to whimper in complaint, and lift her hips off the bed.

His laugh was deep in his throat. He held himself above her, his power going straight to his head, and his rock-hard arousal.

But she stayed quiet, and when he lifted his eyes, looking towards her face, she was glaring at him with pink-faced indignant silence.

"Tell me what you want," he challenged. It wasn't just male ego; this came from deeper with him – the part of him that needed reassurance that this was okay, that she wanted this, that having sex with him wasn't just an act of servitude and obligation.

She glared at him wordlessly, as though the very last thing she intended to do was verbalize her own needs.

He laughed under his breath, then thrust into her, his eyes watching her response, reveling in her obvious relief as his body possessed hers. Her responsiveness though was something he hadn't prepared for.

"You're so damned wet," he groaned, his hands balling in her hair, holding her steady. His eyes bore into hers, hard, tight, demanding. Anyone who knew Malik would have recognized the cold blade of his resolve. Malik was not a man who backed down from anything, as his adversaries had discovered again and again.

"I want you to beg me," he said, simply, his eyes locked to hers.

"Why?" It was a whisper, barely audible.

His expression tightened, his gaze dropped to her lips. "I have no wish to force you to sleep with me," he said, finally, his eyes holding hers. Something passed through her features, a look of comprehension and pity, a pity that made him want to scream, because he'd had enough pity, he'd seen enough sorrow and empathy to last a lifetime.

"You think you're forcing me?"

Her eyes glared back at him. Neither spoke. They simply stared, an intensity in their expressions that was full of flame and defiance.

But Sophia was unlike any woman he'd ever met. Her eyes held his as she lifted her hips, and he didn't pull away, so she drew him into her tight core, and before he could pull out, she wrapped her legs around his hips, holding him there, so deep, so completely buried in her that his head was spinning.

"We have to do this," she said, simply, and once again he felt a surge of determination to remove any idea of duty and obligation from her thoughts. In his mind, he swore every curse he knew, in every language, and then he moved his arousal slowly, small movements, in and out, each one just a gentle thrust, but with a building intensity. Her eyes, still locked to his, morphed, showing surprise, and something akin to confusion, as pleasure and heat overtook her body.

"It is okay, *Sharafaha*," he promised, in his own language. "Feel this. Feel it all."

Her nails clawed his back, her cry animalistic as her muscles squeezed him, her whole body giving way as pleasure exploded through her. She came hard, her orgasm like an earthquake, tearing her apart.

"Oh, god," she moaned, and he stilled, momentarily, fighting an urge to demand she use his name. There'd be time for that. Time to make her beg for him by name, to make her cry his name at the top of her lungs.

He winced as she scratched her hands down his back, undoubtedly scoring marks on his golden flesh.

She was whimpering, pleasure making her voice shrill.

He didn't give her any time to recover.

He thrust into her again, pushing up so he could see the effect on her dainty features, his body tensing with his own needs, which he fought to control. Because he didn't want this to be over.

He rolled onto his back, surprising her, his powerful hands holding her hips, keeping her locked to him, and he lifted her on his length, up and down, driving deeper inside of her, finding new places to pleasure her. She cried out again, not his name, something almost incomprehensible. He shifted a hand to her clit, stroking her and she jerked her head down, her eyes locking to his with a look of such intense passion and need that his own breath burned in his lungs.

Hell, she was gorgeous.

Beneath that innocent veneer, the cool dislike with which she'd always treated him – and he her – there was a wildcat, a woman driven by madness and desire.

He lifted his hands, catching her hair, pulling her head down at the same time he lifted up, kissing her hard, his lips almost punishing on hers, and then he sat up completely, driving himself into her, holding her body tight to his, kissing her, his tongue dueling with hers before dropping to her breasts, biting one nipple first before moving to the other, his fingers lifting and flicking it, rolling it between his forefinger and thumb while his dick drove into her again and again.

She was whimpering on his lap, her head thrown back, her eyes staring heavenward exposing her beautiful throat. His gaze chased sideways, to where he'd caused her flesh to show a pale pink circle, and a rush of power and desire ran through him.

"Please," she cried out, and he wondered if she knew what she was asking for, and how badly he wanted to give it to her? Only he wanted more. He wanted...

He shifted his hips, dislodging her, his eyes unknowingly fierce when they met hers.

"Stand up," he grunted.

Her face showed confusion but she did as he said, scrambling to her feet. He followed swiftly behind, catching her hips and spinning her around, pushing her forwards a little, until her hands were braced on the old timber table above which a tremendous historic mirror hang.

"Watch this. Watch me, watch you." He held her eyes in the mirror as he thrust into her from behind, burying himself so deep inside her, moving his fingers to her front and pleasuring her while he took possession of her again and again and again, thrusting into her until she was crying out with sheer animalistic desire, with the torrent of her sensations and needs.

He stared at her as she began to tip over the edge, as she gave herself over to this completely, and now, he was powerless to stop his own release. He held her hips, driving deep inside her, keeping her arse backed right up to him, and he tipped his seed into her, all of himself, over and over, until he was spent, and she was weak with the shock of her own orgasms.

He clamped a hand around her waist possessively, holding her upright and preventing her from falling forward at the same time, and his eyes locked to hers, challenging her to hold his gaze, challenging her to look away.

She didn't. She stared right back at him, so he saw the awakening that washed over her features, and inside of him, some kind of beast roared.

He had done that to her. He had shown her body what it was capable of and there was still so much more to learn – there was still so much he would teach her.

From the ruins of this situation, from the necessity of their marriage, at least there was this.

SOPHIA FELT as though her cells were pulling her in a thousand directions.

Her senses – every single last one of them – was shimmering inside of her, sparkling and alert, electrified, intensified, startling her with the forcefulness of this sense of pleasure.

There was no escaping her desire.

She stared at Malik, a man she'd always disliked and feared in equal measure, and felt only... need.

She didn't want him to pull out of her; she didn't want her body to lose this closeness and proximity. She wanted... more.

So much more.

Her own desperate hunger for him made her cheeks colour and now, she dropped her gaze, even when she had told herself she wouldn't be the first to look away.

They were in the eye of the storm, though. And it had been a storm – a storm of complete desire, of madness and insanity, and it had been more amazing than she could find any kind of words for – it had blown her away, utterly and completely. She was lost and found, all at once.

But the calm came, and suddenly her nakedness, their

closeness, the passion that was still splitting her breath into tiny little explosions of air, made her self-conscious. With a small sigh, she shifted her body away from his, the desertion of his body from hers like a physical blow. She didn't show that, though. With great effort, she kept her expression neutral, her eyes as cool as she could make them.

"There," she murmured, the word only slightly shaky as she stood with the appearance of confidence. "That wasn't so hard, was it?"

She arched a brow and then turned her back, strolling to the wardrobe and grabbing a robe. She wrapped it around her body, cinching it at the waist.

When she stepped back into the bedroom, he'd pulled his pants back on, but they sat low on his hips, and her eyes were drawn to his broadly muscled chest, his tanned, sculpted body, and her throat was dry suddenly.

Addan had been eleven months older, but he had always said Malik should have been born first. Malik, Addan had insisted, was far more suited to rule. With his cold-hearted ruthlessness, his black and white morality, a strength and determination that were forged from some kind of ancient, kingly fibre, deep inside of him.

She looked at him now and wondered how there could ever have been a world in which he wasn't king?

And if he had been, all along?

This marriage would never have happened.

She would *never* have agreed to this betrothal, no matter how much it had meant to her father and his.

No.

This had all been about Addan.

Her heart lurched and stupid, hot tears filled her eyes. She spun away from him, but not fast enough. She saw the tightening of his jaw, the solidifying of all his features, as he skimmed her face, his eyes absorbing every detail of her response.

"I hurt you?" The words surprised her. Her stomach squeezed because beneath his graveled demand, she heard abhorrence.

He hated the idea of having caused her pain.

She swallowed, shaking her head. "No. Not at all."

His hands on her shoulders were demanding, but gentle. He spun her around and simply stared at her, assessing her. "You are crying."

The noise that escaped her lips was a cross between a laugh and a sob. "Am I?"

A thumb wiped beneath her left eye. "Why?"

She swept her eyes shut for a second, her lashes forming two dark fans against her pale skin.

"It's him, isn't it?"

The words were laced with iron.

There was no point – and no reason – to deny it.

"Yes." She bit down on her lower lip, her eyes still closed. "I just… miss him."

Silence. A tense silence, a silence that sent barbs of wire down her spine.

"As soon as you have conceived my child, we will not need to see each other again. At least, not often."

And he stepped away from her, pacing across the room.

She blinked her eyes open, her gaze landing on his back. She hadn't meant that. She hadn't meant anything. Only her heart was heavy for the man she'd lost, the marriage she'd been supposed to make.

And the power of what she'd shared with her intended fiancé's brother filled her with a sense of shame. Because she'd enjoyed it. Hell, she'd wanted to bottle up the moment and taste it every single day for the rest of her life, to relive that sense of pleasure from now until kingdom come.

Guilt tore through her.

She didn't want to want Malik.

She didn't want to desire him.

It should have been Addan.

She didn't say anything – she didn't offer a word of solace or reassurance. Nor did she seek any from her husband. She turned away from him, her legs not feeling quite steady, picked a book off the shelf and settled herself in an armchair to read. Or, at least, to pretend to.

CHAPTER 3

"*SHARAFAHA, I DREAMED OF YOU* again last night. I dreamed you were here, and I was with you, and we were swimming in the Ocean of Alindor. I dreamed you swam all the way to the bottom and lifted a tiara off the floor, like some kind of ancient Queen, but when you put it on your head, it turned into gold dust and spread through your hair. I guess you could say I miss you! Give Arabella my love and hurry home. Our kingdom awaits. Yours, Rex."

SOPHIA WOKE WITH A START, a heavy sense of disorientation in her gut, followed by that same feeling of blinding grief and realization that had almost strangled her every morning for the last year.

It was the last letter Addan had sent her – signed 'Rex', her pet name for him. She'd read all his letters so many times they were burned into her brain now – which was quite the accomplishment, given there were hundreds of the things.

But how else could she keep Addan alive, than to invoke his words at every opportunity she got?

While he lived, she'd stored them carelessly, tossed into a drawer in her room. Now, with the knowledge that the collection was complete, that no more would be added to its number, she'd had a box made. Gold and pearl, for grief and royalty, it was lined in purple velvet, and had a padlock at its centre. She wore the key on a small chain around her wrist – it was dainty and delicate and to the untrained eye would pass simply as a charm bracelet of sorts.

Wearing it made her feel close to Addan – wearing it was a way back to him.

She sat up straighter, her heart racing, her body feeling oddly alive, strangely heavy and light, and she blinked her eyes into the unfamiliar room. She reached for the key automatically, her fingertips stroking it lightly.

A noise beside her had her gaze shifting and then, it all came flooding back. Memories assaulted her from every direction and a small moan flew from her lips before she could stop it, a sound of remembered pleasure, and of disbelief at how completely entranced she'd been to this sensation, this need.

She couldn't tell if Malik was naked or not, but his chest was exposed, a pale sheet wrapped over his waist. While he slept, she stared, unashamedly devouring his naked body with her eyes, hungrily chasing his flesh, drinking the sight of him up and committing it to her mind.

But looking was dangerous, because it flushed memories through her blood, reminding her of how his chest had felt pressed to her naked breasts, reminding her how his body had felt – heavy and strong above hers.

Looking was problematic because every second she allowed herself to stare was a second that heated her body and filled her with temptation. Looking making her want to touch, to reach out and run a finger over his chest, to drop her mouth to his chest and kiss a trail from one of his nipples to the other, then all the way down to his navel and further down... her eyes moved in that direction and her breath hissed out of her.

The sheet was tented, pushed up as proof of his arousal, even in sleep, impossible to ignore. She clasped her fingers into her palms in an effort not to touch him.

In vain. And unnecessarily.

Because he moved – and quickly – pushing the sheet aside in the same movement that had him kneeling and then straddling her, his kiss pushing her back to the bed, pinning her to the mattress. His hand spread her thighs and then he pushed inside of her, wordlessly, fast, hungrily. She made not a noise, but the storm raged through her, a storm that was alive with a thousand lightning bolts, a storm that transformed her bloodstream and made heat and desire incinerate her cells.

Every possession was purposeful and intense, every beat of his body a mark against her soul, a mark of his possession of her.

Just like he'd coloured the skin of her shoulder, he was marking her invisibly now, inside, leaving little scars of him deep in her being.

But she couldn't care. She couldn't feel anything except abject relief as pleasure spun like a whirlpool and sucked her through its centre. She bit his shoulder as she came, and he drove into her harder, his body so incredibly powerful, her desire like another person in the room.

Even as she came, she felt her needs rising again, she felt an insatiable desire for this and him.

She also felt shock at how unexpected this was, at how little she'd anticipated she might want this.

But, that was a lie, wasn't it?

Her heart twisted as she remembered the second time she'd met Malik. The first had been when she was still a child, too young to be anything but intimidated by the older, powerful prince, the young man, as he'd been then, who'd already been so obviously scathing of the rules, of authority, and of the trappings of royalty.

Then, she'd been in awe of him.

But when, years ago, he'd returned to Abu Faya unexpectedly, and arrived unannounced while Addan was instructing her in the ancient form of Abu Fayan martial arts – *Al antaya* – he'd looked at her in a way that had burned the soles of her feet. He'd looked at her and she'd had the strangest sense that he was undressing her with his eyes, but not just physically. She'd felt like he was stripping away her skin, her muscles and her blood and bones until only the essence of who she was remained. She'd felt more naked in that moment than she ever had before.

He'd been dismissive – no, he'd been downright rude. He'd spoken to Addan in Abu Fayan, perhaps not realizing she could speak it fluently.

"So this is your foreign bride, brother?"

"Her name is Sophia," Addan had responded calmly, in that way he had – with strength and softness all at once. "And you will treat her with respect."

"She is pretty, I suppose, but no more so than any number of princesses you could have wed. Why this woman?"

Sophia had felt her insides fill with ice and she'd sworn to dislike this man from that moment onwards.

"Because I love her," Addan had answered in English, turning to face Sophia with a slow wink. "And because there is no one on earth, princess or otherwise, who will make a better queen for our people."

Malik had left, and while Addan's words had buoyed her, Malik's judgment had sat within her like a stone. Each time she'd seen him after that, she'd remembered his disappointment and derision. While he'd paid lip service to respecting her, his manner had always reeked of disapproval, leaving her in little doubt that his first assessment hadn't altered with time.

He couldn't understand why Addan was marrying her – and now it was even worse, for he'd had to endure that fate personally.

He thrust into her again and she crashed back to the present, to the windswept coastline of their desire, her eyes wide when they met his. Sleepiness surrounded them, still whispering in the night air, and the ancient tower was filled with the tang of salt and heat, the humidity and spices for which this country was famed.

He rolled his hips and she bit down on her lips, his name heavy in her mouth. It pushed against her tongue, rolled over her teeth, saturated her lips, but she would not speak it. She wouldn't give him the satisfaction of hearing her beg for him over and over, even when his name was thundering through her blood stream.

Her eyes showed defiance even as waves of pleasure broke upon her soul, even as she welcome the collapse of resistance, as she welcomed all of this.

She arched her back, drowning in her body's needs and he grabbed her, lifting her up, holding her tight to his chest as he came inside of her, his own body wracked with the strength of his release, his voice deep and guttural.

Her breathing was as forced as if she'd run a mile at speed, her lungs burning from the intensity. She clung to him – spent and exhausted – her body satisfied while her mind was spinning, trying to make sense of this feeling, this pleasure, this strange, pervasive hunger.

He pulled out of her, and moved to his side of the bed, lying on his back.

Sophia looked at him, her eyes running over his profile.

"Go to sleep, *Sharafaha*. It's the middle of the night."

The middle of her wedding night. She swallowed, the lump in her throat heavy and constricting. She searched for something to say – anything – but he rolled over, turning his back to her, and silence descended once more.

If she'd known what point she wanted to make, she would have woken him up, but she was a tangle of confusion. She lay down, rolling to her side of the bed, staring at the ancient stonewalls of this room, cast in a milky, silver moonlight, and tried not to think.

Not to think of Addan and the way they'd laughed about this tradition. She tried not to think about whether she could have walked away from this marriage, this obligation, and gone back to her real life.

But what was her real life?

Since childhood, she'd been groomed for this role, she'd believed it to be her fate. She spoke Abu Fayan and two dialects of the Bedouin tribes, she knew everything there was to know about the history and culture of this proud and prosperous nation. And what was there for her at home? A mother who'd hastily married a man much younger than herself? A sister who was busy raising her own family?

Or marriage to Malik, a man she knew little about save for one vital, salient fact: Addan had adored him. Addan had believed him to be the best of men, and she trusted Addan unstintingly. She therefore trusted that this marriage would, in time, make some kind of sense.

A pit opened up in her heart, though, and she suspected it would never be full.

WHEN HE WOKE, the sun had crested over the dunes in the distance, bathing the white stone walls of this turret in pale peaches and gold. He'd always loved this time of day, for the magic that draped itself around the world, whispering secrets of decades long since past.

He loved this time of day for its faithfulness, its service, for the fact the palette hadn't changed at all since his childhood.

He woke up feeling like he could do anything, as though he were all powerful. The feelings were familiar to Malik – sex always left him with this sense of utter satiation and egotism. Good sex was even better.

And last night had been some of the best sex of his life.

A rock seemed to drop through him, thudding in his chest. Because he hadn't just slept with a beautiful woman, a random woman, a royal groupie, a willing lover keen for a night in the bed of the Sheikh.

He'd slept with Addan's fiancé. He'd taken the virginity of the woman his brother had loved.

And he would do it again and again and again, given the chance.

His insides churned as he turned to look at her and disgust –self-disgust – rolled through him. Fast asleep, she looked so much younger than she was. Her blonde hair was loose, tumbling about her shoulders in glorious waves, her cheeks were pink, even in her sleep, and her little cupid's bow lips were parted slightly.

"You don't know her like I do," Addan had said, his smile enigmatic as he'd surveyed the view of the desert's primary oasis. Palm trees curved around one edge, and wild camels drank greedily at its edge.

Malik had picked up a stone and cast it over the water's surface, his expression grim. "I beg your pardon, I have known plenty of women like Sophia Howard."

Addan's laugh had filled the space, causing one of their Arabian stallions to beat its hooves in disapproval. "You think so?"

"She is just a silly American girl."

Addan had shaken his head. "You are determined not to like her, and that saddens me, brother. But I know you well enough to know I cannot change your mind once you have made it." His eyes had narrowed with that quiet determination of his. "Only promise me, as my brother and my subject, that you will keep your feelings to yourself. She is valuable to me, valuable to this country, and she is more sensitive than she seems. I will not have her upset because you think she is just like one of your cheap lovers…"

Malik's gut tightened now. He'd promised Addan he would never let Sophia know how he felt. He'd promised his brother, his best friend, a man he adored and admired, that he would keep his feelings to himself.

And he had.

Every last one of them. He'd travelled more and more, stayed away from his home increasingly often, and he'd put Sophia and her mysterious silver blue eyes from his mind.

And now, his body was hard for her, despite the fact he'd taken her in the middle of the night, driving into her and burning them both with the intensity of his need.

Hell.

This was a problem. He jack-knifed out of bed, moving to the small kitchen area and quietly fixing himself a coffee. While it brewed, the smell of spicy caffeine filling the small room, he pulled on a pair of pants and tied his hair up in a knot on the top of his head. As soon as the cup had filled, he grabbed it and strode towards the parapet balcony, stepping out and breathing in the desert air with relief.

He would need to sleep with her often, until she had conceived. Then, he could leave her to the care of his servants, blowing into the desert just as he always had, taking himself out amongst his people, seeing her as infrequently as ever. He'd made an art form of ignoring her – how long had it been since he'd decided that was the safest course of action?

When their child was born, he would need to come back, of course.

For a time.

But he would control his desire for her. He would maintain a respectful distance.

She had been Addan's fiancé, his chosen bride.

This was just sex – for the sake of the royal line.

And what of his libido, which he'd delighted in indulging often?

His expression tightened, his eyes skimming the dunes in the distance. He wouldn't go without sex. He was a man, and a man who had become used to indulging his body's needs. His great grandfather had dispensed with the harem, something Malik had often joked to Addan about with mock regret. He didn't want a harem.

But he would need a mistress.

Someone discreet. Someone who…

His stomach rolled at the idea of sleeping with anyone else, a visceral rejection to the notion ricocheting through him.

He didn't want anyone else. In that moment, despite the fact he'd filled his bed with supermodels, actresses, heiresses, princesses and renowned beauties in the past, despite the fact he knew he could snap his fingers and have any one of them back in his life, he knew he wouldn't.

He stared out at the desert and the true consequences of his situation exploded through him for the first time.

He was not a man who would cheat.

Having pledged himself to this woman, he knew he would stay faithful to her.

Which meant celibacy.

He couldn't sleep with her for any reason other than procreation.

And he wouldn't cheat on her.

So he would have to learn to curb his libido.

The idea was as unpalatable as any he'd known. He ground his teeth together, drinking his coffee, knowing that unpleasant as the notion was, he would do it. For what other choice did he have?

She slept late and woke ravenous. Sitting up in bed, her blonde hair unknowingly wild about her petite face, the sheet clasped under her arms, firm across her breast, she scanned the room looking for any sign of Malik.

There was none.

Breathing a small sigh of relief, she wrapped the sheet more firmly around herself, wedging her way out of bed and walking as best she could in such a tight makeshift dress towards the coffee machine. It was lukewarm, but not hot. So he was awake – and fueled with caffeine. She pressed the button to reheat it and moved towards the balcony, drawn by the brightness and warmth of the day.

The sight of her husband arrested her completely.

He was naked from the waist up, his body so firmly muscled, so toned and strong, that she could only stare. The sun danced across his honeyed flesh, showing the angles and planes of his sculpted chest. Her heart raced when his eyes moved to hers, and she was powerless to look away, even when her pulse was hammering and her heart slamming into her ribs.

"You slept late," he murmured, his gaze trailing down her body as though she were naked.

"Not if you subtract how much of last night I spent awake."

For the briefest moment, she thought she saw amusement flicker across his face, a hint of laughter in his eyes, but it was extinguished almost instantly.

"There is food inside," he murmured. "If you are hungry."

She was. Ravenous.

But her stomach's needs were taking a backseat to other more pressing imperatives. She looked at her husband and felt a tightening in the ball of her stomach, a burst of need that was so powerful she knew she wouldn't be able to ignore it – so powerful she wasn't sure she *wanted* to ignore it.

Her eyes lifted to his, helplessly, her tongue darting out to the corner of her mouth as she swallowed.

They were here for one reason, and one reason only: to beget an heir.

Shifting a little, her eyes sparking now with a silent challenge, she loosened the sheet from beneath her arms, dropping it to the floor. "Food can wait."

He stormed across the small balcony, scooping her up and carrying her inside, his eyes burning into hers, raking over her expression, his own need as insatiable as her own. He lay her down on the mattress and stood for a moment, staring at her nakedness, her beautiful body bearing the marks of his intimacy, her pale flesh marked red in parts from his stubble, his touch, his kiss, her lips swollen from his kisses, her nipples engorged, begging him to take them in his mouth and hands once more.

He parted her legs wordlessly, his eyes boring into hers, as he straddled her, his cock at the apex of her thighs. She held her breath, her body stilled. He watched her for a moment and then drove himself into her feminine depths, his body tightening at the sweet little moaning sounds she made.

And it occurred to him that in this one way, they were

almost designed for each other. He'd had a lot of sex with a lot of women, and he could honestly say not one of them had driven him quite as wild as his innocent wife: his brother's bride.

Her heart would always belong to another man, but Sophia's delectable body was all his – and, despite the circumstances, Malik was glad for that. He hated that he was, he hated that he felt anything other than duty as he drove into his wife, as he thrust himself deep into her body and held her tight, her pleasure driving her wild. He hated that he felt anything for her, but he couldn't deny it: on some level, he was actually glad to be married to her, glad he could do this whenever passion overtook them, glad it was his body doing this to hers.

Which, Malik accepted, made him just about the worst bastard known to man.

CHAPTER 4

MALIK TAPPED HIS FINGERS against the edge of the table, his expression grim. Anyone who knew the powerful ruler would clearly see he was in a mood. But not many would guess the reason for it.

It had been eight days since they'd left the tower in the sky. Eight days in which urgent business with a desert tribe had called him away from the palace and his bride. Eight days riding across the vast rolling sand dunes of Abu Faya, a powerful steed between his legs, sand, heat and lukewarm water testing his patience almost as much as an all-consuming hunger for the woman whose innocence he'd taken nights before.

"You cannot prevent anyone from your tribe from attending university," he spoke with a calmness he didn't feel. Desert winds flapped the sides of the tent. The afternoon was closing in; he wanted this wrapped up. He wouldn't spend another night out here, restless and craving a woman who was thousands of miles from him.

He would go home and have sex with his wife, whether this business was resolved or not. True, it was his duty to be here, to oversee this conflict, but it was also his duty to provide Abu Faya with an heir, and that was something he considered to be a matter of life and death.

Telling himself his compulsion to return to his marital bed had more to do with creating an heir than it did his desire for his wife, he homed his attention back on the meeting. The tribe leader was watching him, a glint of iron in the man's eyes. Malik recognized it well – he wore the same determination, the same certainty that he alone knew what was best for his people.

Suppressing a sigh, he leaned forward, refilling the other man's glass of *Anäsh-haba* wine. It was a gesture that didn't go unrecognized by those in attendance. For the Sheikh of Abu Faya to serve a tribal leader was a gesture of great deference and respect.

And Malik did respect Laith.

Before he'd inherited Addan's title, he'd looked upon the older man almost as a father figure, and certainly as a friend. They butted heads more now, Laith's desire to rule his tribe oftentimes in conflict with Malik's wishes for the country.

"You are worried you will lose your young," he said, with understanding. "That each teenager who leaves this way of life, to take up another, to study in the cities and discover that modern existence for themselves will dilute the ways of your ancient people."

Laith's eyes widened; he dipped his head in silent concession. "We cannot survive if our numbers continue to be diminished."

"I know this," Malik lifted his wine, taking a sip of the sweet, refreshing drink before fixing Laith with a direct stare. "And I sympathise with your position. But you cannot keep your people hostage to this desert. Times are not what they were a hundred, or even fifty, years ago. Healthcare,

education, dentistry, human rights – there is an homogeniza-
tion of these requirements."

"We do not want it."

Malik shook his head, his temper rising. "Do not lie to
me, old man. I saw your fear when your grandson was diag-
nosed with leukemia. You availed yourself of the best
medical care our nation could offer, you did not leave his
health to ancient proverbs and herbal treatments."

Laith bared his teeth but made a grunt of concession.
"Health is different."

"This woman wants to study law. She wants to move to
the city to take up her degree. You cannot forbid her from
doing so; you cannot punish and threaten to exile her
parents if she goes. What kind of community do you lead if
your people are beholden to you out of fear rather than
respect?"

Laith's demeanour didn't shift. "Are you ordering me to
allow this?"

Malik sat back in the chair, casting his eyes about the
table. On one side, sat members of his own government and
security delegation, liaisons to the Bedouin communities that
peppered these deserts. On the other sat members of Laith's
tribe, as well as delegates from other communities, interested
in the outcome of these speeches.

"I am reluctant to interfere in your governance." He drank
his wine. "I have deep respect for you, your people and your
way of life." He turned his head, staring through the flap of
the tent, towards the wild, unfettered desert. "There have
been many times in my life when I wished to live amongst
you."

Laith's voice was crackled by age when he spoke. "And we
have always welcomed you."

Malik's eyes swept shut as he remembered that detail –
the times when he ran from the palace to this community,

living beneath the stars, their simple life appealing to something ancient and strong within his soul. The weeks after Addan's death had required him to be at the palace, but as soon as life had appeared to return to normal, he'd come to Laith, to the desert, to grieve without the confines of staff, without the expectation that he would know just what to say and how to act to everyone, at all times.

"I chose to come to you," he said slowly. "I have always chosen to spend time here, with you, like this, when I could. Despite all that is at my fingertips – the immense wealth of my family, the power of my position, the love of my brother, I have come to the desert tribes and chosen to partake in this way of life." He turned his head back to Laith. "We are not men of the city, Laith."

He felt the men on both sides shift, some nodding, some murmuring under their breath. He spoke quietly, but with the effortless command and strength that were very much a part and parcel of this man's being. "We are not a people born to live in comfort, with technology making our lives easy and convenient. Give me a modern city and I feel a prisoner," he muttered. "This," he swept his hand, encompassing the canvas tent and the rugs at their feet, "is my idea of a home. The stars are the only lights I want at night, a horse the transport I prefer, the sound of ancient songs and spoken histories what I want to dance to and listen to as I fall asleep. This is a part of who we are. Men, women and children of Abu Faya carry the sands of the desert in their skin, in their cells; these are our ways."

More noise, some clapping of hands and nodding.

"You must trust that this woman, and others like her, will feel a pull back to this way of life. You must believe there is strength and passion in us, that draws us to these deserts."

Laith's expression was taut.

"And still," Malik continued, "you must let her go."

There was silence around the table now, but it was a silence of understanding, of acceptance. All but Laith saw that Malik was right, and even Laith was softening. "I will think on it," he said finally, lifting his cup and holding it towards Malik in a silent gesture of respect. "And I thank you, Sheikh, for coming to me at this time. Your counsel is, as ever, appreciated."

Malik stayed only so long as he felt absolutely necessary and then climbed onto his horse, his gaze set in the distance – beyond which was his palace, and his bride.

He would ride through the night.

His security detail wouldn't like it, but Malik had little care for that.

———

Sophia smiled as she watched the children, their frivolity and laughter transcending geography and culture. These children, playing in the courtyard of their school, reminded her so completely of herself and Bella as children. They ran from one side of the space to the other, flicking water from the fountain and laughing when the droplets landed on their uniforms. It was a searingly hot day, quite unbearable. She wished, for a moment, she could forget the fact she was on an official visit, to launch the new technology lab of this government-run school, to forget the fact there were photographers lined up from international newspapers, ready to capture her every move. She wished she could forget for a moment that she was Sheikha Sophia and join in the water fight, splashing herself, cooling herself down.

Despite the heat of the day, though, it wasn't that alone which had caused Sophia to feel over-hot.

Hers was a heat that came from inside, a heat generated in the blood that was pounding through her body, making her heart race and her pulse gush. It was a heat that Malik had set alight, that was ravaging her completely.

She kept her smile in place, nodding as the headmistress continued to explain the operations of the school.

The children were adorable.

Out of nowhere, the image came to her of another little person, a baby born to her and Malik, and for a second, her smile almost dropped. Because, in her mind's eye, she could see that child so clearly! The smile, the dimples, the dark hair like his, the inquiring eyes, the easy smile.

Her heart skidded in her chest.

Was it possible that little baby was already growing inside her?

Her fingertips tingled and she fought an impulse to run a hand over her flat stomach.

She was familiar enough with the global media's intense interest in her life to know that such a gesture would headline international papers and websites if she were to succumb to it.

And so she stood still, nodding and smiling, picture-perfect and dying with impatience.

She knew only that Malik had been called away urgently. The minute they'd descended from the tower, real life had absorbed them back into it. For a day, they'd escaped, they'd become intimately acquainted with one another's bodies, and then one of his ministers had approached him, speaking quietly and in a dialect she didn't recognize. Malik's expression had darkened, his skin paled, and then he'd turned to face her.

He hadn't smiled. "Urgent business requires my attention."

"Oh." A stupid rejoinder, but she hadn't known what to say; she hadn't been prepared for the intense rejection she'd feel at the very idea that he was to go away again. How could her body have become dependent on his in such a short space of time? "Why? Where?"

She'd kicked herself for giving voice to the needy questions.

He'd frowned, perhaps feeling her intrusion was unwelcome. "Deep into the desert, to the south." It was clear he was already mentally there. "I cannot say how long I will be away."

And he'd turned and left, without any further goodbye. What had she expected? A passionate kiss or embrace in front of his staff and hers? A long, detailed conversation? An accounting for his time?

Addan and she had been best friends. When the tribes had flared up and required Addan's attention, he'd talked to Sophia about it at length. He'd seen her as an asset to him, recognizing that the daughter to a US senator and a woman practically raised to be Sheikha, with a passion for the classics, knew more than a little bit about politics and human nature.

She wondered which of the tribes was calling Malik away, and for what reason.

And she reconciled herself to the fact Malik might not see their marriage as Addan had – he might not wish her to be a queen who involved herself on the political side.

Well, tough.

She wasn't just window dressing. Addan had known her, he'd understood. Sophia wanted to make a difference in the world, to be an instrument of change. It was one of the main reasons she'd agreed to sacrifice personal privacy and take up this very visible, high-profile position within the Abu Fayan royal family.

There was no information forthcoming about Malik's trip, nor if he was seeing success.

Frustration gnawed at her gut, but she quelled it. This

was still the first week of their marriage. They were yet to find any kind of groove – he had no idea what she wanted and that was her fault. She hadn't told him.

The year of their betrothal had seen them together on only a handful of occasions and his coldness to her had made any kind of conversation almost impossible, just as it had for the duration of their acquaintance.

But now, there was no coldness. Only white hot heat, and she had to get past the feeling that she was an unwanted bride and navigate their relationship – to get what she needed out of this royal life.

As soon as she arrived back at the palace, as dusk was curdling the sky pink and purple and gold was dipping down towards the distant oceans, Sophia made a beeline for the private residence.

She hadn't moved into their bedroom.

The bedroom she was to share with Malik.

With him away immediately after the wedding, it hadn't felt right somehow. Besides, she preferred it here, in her little sanctuary, the bedroom that was next to Addan's, the suite they'd sat up in and talked about everything and anything until all hours of the morning.

This felt like home. She wasn't ready to give it up yet.

She stripped naked and pulled a pair of bathers from the wardrobe, the white bikini a gift from some designer or other. Sophia donated most of the fashionable gifts she was sent – there were too many for her to ever wear and she knew that they were better being auctioned, the money going towards good causes.

For some reason, this pair of swimmers had avoided that fate.

The pool beyond her bedroom could only be accessed by the royal family, and only through their bedrooms. It was a completely private space, and she reveled in that – she reveled in knowing that here, at least, she could be unobserved. She could be herself.

There was no relief from the heat of the day, nor the fever in her blood.

She dove into the pool without preamble, smiling as the water enveloped her, as it cooled her flesh and relaxed her mind. She kicked hard underwater, swimming the length, pushing up only when she reached the opposite end.

Here, she paused a moment before diving back underwater and doing a summersault, and then another.

As a child, she'd harboured fantasies of joining the American synchronized swimming team and going to the Olympics. She'd outgrown the dream but not the love of playing in the water.

She laughed when she burst through the surface and then moved to the edge, bracing her arms against the sun-warmed coping, staring out at the sky. This time of day was like magic. As the sun waned to accommodate the moon, the blanket of stars darkening, coming closer, whispering secrets of the evening. She felt as though she was a celestial being, for those few moments where day and night were completely merged.

She spun around slowly in the water, chasing the sky, but an incongruous shape caught her attention and she jerked her head in that direction.

Only to feel like her heart had been exploded in her chest. Draped against the wall opposite, his dark eyes watching her with an intensity she couldn't comprehend, was Malik.

Broad, big, wild Malik, dragged in from the deserts, his expression impossible to read, his eyes trained on her with an intensity that stole her breath. Even as she turned to face him, he continued to stare at her, and her lips parted of their own accord, breath still almost impossible to find.

So, he was back.

He looked... the least regal she'd ever seen him. Wearing the traditional white robes of Abu Faya, they were crinkled and dusted by sand. His hair was loose, around his shoulders, knotted and tangled. Despite this, he was more handsome than ever.

She stared.

She stared without realizing it and then when she did, she didn't stop. She couldn't.

It had been over a week without him and her body was at a fever pitch of desire.

He didn't say a word, but she felt his invitation. She felt his command, and it sent thrills down her spine.

One slightly arched brow was all it took.

She swam through the water, her stride confident and easy, and before she could second-guess what she was doing, she stepped out of the pool, her eyes not leaving his face.

She saw the moment he realised what she was wearing, the way his eyes dragged down her body, taking in every curve and plane, every divot of skin, every single bit of her. He dragged his gaze over her body and she felt... naked. In the best possible way.

When she was only a step away from him, he closed the distance, pushing up from the wall and striding forwards. Their bodies touched. Electricity sparked.

"You're back," she said needlessly.

He didn't respond.

She swallowed, breathing in deeply, inhaling his intoxicating, musky scent, her insides quivering. Her feline eyes watched him, waiting, every cell in her body stagnant, still, hungry.

The air around them seemed to be thick, frozen with time. He stared down at her, his dark eyes flecked with gold towards the centre, rimmed with dark, curling lashes.

He was big and wild, untamable. The word came to her from nowhere but it was so apt.

She swallowed, her heart racing in her chest.

His eyes dropped to her lips and they parted on a soft exhalation.

She didn't understand the words he spoke next. Deep and guttural, and from a dialect she'd never heard, much less been taught. Was it the same he'd used when they were making love and he'd whispered in her ear, words she didn't understand but instinctively felt?

They were magical words, deep and throaty, and they called to something buried far down in her chest.

She heard the words and stared at him, her pulse ricocheting like crazy through her body.

And then he kissed her, without preamble, as though he couldn't resist.

It was a kiss that was born of fire and flame, a kiss that was born of absolute necessity, as though without it, all the oxygen on earth would drain away.

His hand curved around her wet head, his fingers splayed across her scalp, pulling her head back a little, angling her to allow his mouth maximum access.

She groaned, a noise that curled through her throat.

He was wearing too many clothes. Her hands found his shirt and pulled at it, but he shook his head, his eyes holding warning.

"I must shower." There was reluctance in the words. Reluctance and frustration. She felt the proof of his desire, hard against her belly.

"Shower?" The hint of a delay wasn't welcome. She refuted it instantly. "Shower later."

He groaned and she felt his desperation and yes, fear, because he too was as driven by this desire as she was – as held hostage to it is as anything else in life ever had been.

"I have been riding for twenty hours," he said, shaking his head. "I need to shower, and sleep…"

"But you came to see me," she said pointedly, her hands reaching inside his shirt despite his protest, curving around his hips. She stroked his flesh there and then dipped them lower, into the waistband of his pants. His eyes swept closed and his Adam's apple bobbed as he swallowed.

"I came to shower," he insisted, "and sleep."

He lifted his hands to her breasts, covering them indolently, possessively, lazily, feeling the weight of them in his palms.

Her breath was tight, burning inside her lungs.

"Yet you're here…"

His eyes narrowed, and his fingers lifted to the straps of her bathers. Watching her, waiting for her to say something, perhaps to demur, he slid the straps lower. She shivered as they ran over her arms, and he dragged them lower still, revealing her breasts completely to his proprietary inspection. "I heard you splashing."

She bit down on her lower lip, her body swaying forward slightly in an unspoken invitation. "You should have joined me."

His eyes dropped to her breasts now, to where his fingers were curved around her flesh. She let out a whimper as he took one nipple between his forefinger and thumb, rolling it and increasing his pressure until she moaned, tilting her head back, staring at a sky that was growing darker by the minute.

"Don't shower," she pleaded, not even remotely ashamed to beg that of him. "Not yet."

His eyes lifted to her face, and there was a battle being waged inside of him. A war of control, a fight for sanity.

"I must." He gave her nipple one last squeeze, tight, and

her gut kicked in response, her insides slicking with moist heat.

Her pulse was a livewire.

"Then why don't I come and wash you," she murmured, wondering at this heady sense of power she felt, this certainty that he wouldn't say 'no' to what she was offering.

Their eyes met once more and desire exploded between them.

The battle he was waging shifted. "If you wish, *Sharafaha*."

CHAPTER 5

H IS BODY WAS SO broad and powerful. She could easily believe he was the kind of man who'd been conjured from the ancient myths of this historic land. Myths that spoke of beasts being cast to human form, that spoke of men being forged from the depths of the ocean or the bowels of the desert, men who could withstand sandstorm and earthquakes and duel with the gods.

Even though this was her suggestion, she was nervous now, uncertain. She reached for a sponge and layered spiced body wash on it, buying for time. His look showed he understood that, that he was aware of her hesitation.

He stretched his arms out wide, and unconsciously she bit down on her lower lip, scanning his ridged abdomen and arms that were thick and sculpted. On the underside of his left bicep, he had a scrawling tattoo. She held the sponge in her hand and traced it with her fingertip, reading the words now.

الظلام ضوء الولادات

SHE FROWNED, translating the words into her native English. "Darkness births light?"

His chest stilled as his breath caught in his lungs. "You speak and read Abu Fayan with ease."

It wasn't praise, so much as an observation.

Her smile was lopsided, and only the work of an instant. "I've lived here a long time."

"Yes."

Her eyes lifted to his. "When did you get it done?"

"A while ago."

She swallowed, emotions balling inside her. "After Addan?"

There was something in his eyes when he turned to face her. "No." Something stony and cold. Something like rejection.

"When?" She persisted.

His expression tightened, if that was even possible. "Why do you think any one particular event led to my tattoo?"

Another smile flitted across her face. She lifted the loofah and began to rub his shoulders, moving slowly even when it was obviously a torment for him, even when their mutual desire was pulsing between them, demanding indulgence.

"It's not a picture of an anchor or an eagle," she quipped. "It's a profound statement. Of course it was inspired by something."

He was quiet, and she wondered if he was going to answer. Then, as she moved around to his back, sponging his flesh there, marveling at his firmly muscled skin, he spoke. "After my father's death."

She sighed. "It was devastating."

"He'd been sick a while," Malik murmured.

"Yes," Sophia swept her eyes shut, remembering what that

sickness looks like. "But that doesn't make it any easier." Her fingers curved to his hips and around to his front. He stilled as the loofah brushed the ridges of his abdomen, low down, curving close to his powerful erection.

His hand curved over hers, holding it for a moment, and her breath jammed in her throat. "You were a child when your father died?"

She nodded, but he couldn't see her, so Sophia cleared her throat. "Yes." She moved around to his front, their eyes locking. "And darkness was everywhere." She sponged his shoulder, memories of that time heavy in her mind.

"It was very sudden, with your father," he murmured, lifting a hand and stroking her hair, the gesture surprising her.

"It was." Her lips pulled into a small grimace. "Mercifully so." His hand dropped to her shoulder. "I was only a child but I remember feeling like the walls of my world had crashed down on me, like I'd never be the same again. He was so dynamic; so incredibly special." She sighed softly. "I couldn't understand how someone could simply cease to exist."

"I have felt the same each time I have lost someone I loved." He focused on a point over her shoulder, his expression grim. "With my father, he was such a force of energy."

"That's the perfect way to describe him."

Malik's eyes dropped to hers, and something fired in her belly – desire and need, certainty and a billion questions that bubbled just beneath the surface.

"When he was young," Malik murmured, "the country was very different. There had been civil war in his lifetime, and he'd seen the ravages of that on our country. He was a skilled statesman and a clever politician."

"And a wonderful man," she added, her expression wistful as she blinked away from Malik, smoothing the loofah over his flat, toned belly. "I adored your father."

"I know."

There was something in those words, something that spoke almost of disapproval. "You were like a daughter to him."

"He used to call me *Amyrat Saghira*."

"Did he?" The question came from deep inside of him, the words flecked with disapproval.

She blinked, wondering at the strength of his response.

"As a child, I just thought they were pretty words. They used to chase each other around my head like an incantation of a dance." She smiled distractedly. "But then, as I got older, I understood." She placed the loofah on the shelf, her hands bare. "What he wanted, what my father wanted…"

"And that was for you to marry into this family, to become a part of Abu Faya?"

She nodded slowly, a frown creasing her brow. "Yes."

"And what did *you* want, Sophia?"

It was one of the first times he'd used her name, instead of the title *Sharafaha*. It did something strange to her body, making her spine tingle and her knees weak. He said it softly, with an emphasis on the first syllable, like "soff-eah."

She liked it, more than she wanted to.

"I loved this country from the first time I visited," she said quietly. "But it was Addan who made it feel like another home."

Something flickered in his gaze, emotions that were dark and forbearing, yet she barely registered them.

"I felt like I lost everything when dad died. My mother became distant and Bella went to live in Spain with her godparents. I went from having this incredible family to being quite alone."

"Except for Addan?" Malik murmured, the question cold.

"Yes." She bit down on her lower lip. "I don't know why he was so kind to me."

"Don't you?" The question was layered with unspoken answers.

She frowned. "It felt like we'd met before."

A muscle jerked in Malik's jaw. He reached behind Sophia then, shutting off the water. "Enough."

She blinked. "Enough?"

"I do not wish to speak of Addan with you, Sophia."

Sophia's heart turned over and regret filled her. Of course he didn't. Malik had lost his mother, father and now his brother – he knew so much of loss. Why would he want to speak about it, and in that moment? "I'm…"

Before she could finish her sentence, he scooped her up out of the shower and hoisted her over his shoulder, carrying her through the bathroom. He grabbed a towel as they passed, wrapping it over her bare back, and then placed her feet on the floor. She looked around.

His bedroom.

"You have not been sleeping here."

She shook her head slowly. "It didn't feel right."

"Why not? You are my wife. You don't think your place is here, with me?"

She shrugged her slender shoulders. "You haven't been here."

He rubbed the towel over her flesh, drying her, and he wasn't gentle – nothing had ever felt better, though. Her breasts were so sensitive, between her legs was warm and wet. She stifled a moan as he brushed the towel there.

"Whether I am here or not, you should be."

She opened her mouth to fight him but he kissed her, a dazzling kiss of pure possession, of absolute need and fire. He kissed her with all the flame in his body and she surrendered to it and him immediately, an ancient, desperate need firing her senses, filling her with an absolute fever pitch of lust.

Her hands ran over his body, reaching his arousal and cupping his hard length, feeling his strength in her hands.

"You are my wife."

The words were discordant, and seemed to come to her from a long way away. Sophia, always a fighter, responded with light sarcasm.

"No kidding. I was there when we married."

The words caused his expression to tighten, if anything. He moved his body, guiding her back to the bed. She fell onto it unceremoniously and his own frame, so large and powerful, was on top of hers. His hands caught her wrists in them, lifting them above her head, pinning them to the mattress easily. He parted her thighs and thrust into her, deep, hard, so she arched her back, welcoming him and this.

Every movement of his body was a beating of a drum, a call that her spirit answered, a primal, physical need she couldn't help but respond to. Six nights since they'd made love and her body was craving his.

She whimpered as he moved deeper, and then his mouth dropped from her lips to her breasts, his tongue swirling her nipples, sucking one peach aureole deep into his mouth rolling it with his tongue, flicking it before pressing his teeth into her sensitive softness, before transferring to the other breast. His fingers tormented the nipple he'd first kissed, plucking it, rolling it between his forefinger and thumb until she was moaning and whimpering, pleasure thick in her voice.

She lifted her legs, wrapping them behind his back but he caught them at the ankles, pushing them over his shoulders and straightening, staring down at her, his eyes watchful as his body drove hers to the point of explosion.

It was fast and satisfying. Just as soon as she tumbled over the abyss, delight and euphoria erupting from her, he followed after, his own guttural cry in his native tongue, deep and rumbling.

Their panting, torn breaths split the room afterwards. She lay beneath him, her body weakened and strengthened, her mind spinning.

"Well," she said, to break the silence, as he stayed where he was, his powerful frame atop hers, his head dipped so she couldn't make out his expression. "You're back."

But something had shifted. It was as though there'd been a terrible dark storm building between them, and sleeping together had burst it open, breaking rain upon the earth and now there was just relief.

Her fingers trailed the length of his back, lightly, and she felt his body pull in response. Her power was intoxicating.

"How was your trip?" The words were husky, coated with desire.

"Long. And not satisfying." He pushed up so his eyes could stare into the depths of hers and something inside Sophia squeezed.

"Where were you?"

"The plains to the west."

It was a cryptic, unsatisfying response.

"Yes, I gathered," she murmured, surprised to feel a sardonic smile tilting her lips. "But with the *Lakani* people? Or the *Shaman*?"

At that, his eyes flared a little wider and she felt as though he was contemplating ignoring her question, not answering her. With a hint of reluctance, her said, "The *Jakari*."

"Ah. Laith is the ruler of that tribe, isn't he?"

Malik's expression tightened with disapproval. Only for an instant, but enough for Sophia to see it. "Yes."

"And something's happened now?"

He didn't answer.

Sophia sighed. "Addan used to talk to me, Malik." She

THE SHEIKH'S INHERITED BRIDE | 67

lifted a hand and stroked his cheek thoughtfully, feeling the ridges of his facial structure and the stubble of his hair through her fingertips. "I think if you were to do the same, you'd find I could be helpful."

His laugh was spontaneous. A gruff sound of disagreement. "You?" He captured her hand in his and laced his fingers through it, holding it to her side. He pushed up a little higher, so he could see her better. "And tell me, my American, virgin wife," he brought his mouth to her nipple, flicking it with his tongue, tracing the dark aureole so her breath caught in her throat. "What do you think you could teach me about my own people?" He moved to her other breast, inflicting the same delightful torment on her sensitive nerve endings there. "What insight do you have to offer?"

Hurt flexed inside her but she pushed it aside. Sophia had always been a fighter and despite the torrent of sensation he was raining down on her, she fought his words now. "I think you'd be surprised."

His eyes showed his disagreement.

He dragged his lips higher, to the flesh of her décolletage, his tongue flicking the pulse point there. She moaned softly, but wouldn't be derailed.

"Why?" The word was uneven. "Is it so impossible to think I might have a perspective to offer that could be of value to you?"

"You have many things to offer me," he said, moving his hips so she could feel that he was hard again. But his words were unwelcome. His words made her feel that this was somehow cheap and two-dimensional. Like sex was simply sex, and beyond that, he wanted nothing from her.

"Are you saying you want me to be the kind of wife who's waiting for you in bed at the end of the day but doesn't otherwise bother you?"

His lips twisted but his only other response was to thrust

his hips once more. "You say that as though it is not what you want."

"It's not."

She pressed her palms to his chest, her expression serious enough to still him. He held himself above her, watching her, his own features carefully muted of any feeling.

"I'm your wife." She expelled the words slowly, carefully, trying to rein her temper in. She'd learned as a child that her quickness to anger was only a benefit if she could control that anger, if she could mete it out slowly rather than letting it explode in one violent surge of passion, but she was furious. From when she'd been a very young child, and her own family had been ripped apart, she swore she'd have a perfect marriage, a real family, all of her own one day. One that would never fall apart. "We're supposed to be a team. Do you think you need to do all this on your own?"

He stared at her for several long seconds, and she was conscious of his possession of her body, conscious of how badly she wanted to pause this conversation and feel what he could give her, feel that pleasure and euphoric release.

"You are my wife," he said, finally, and now he rolled his hips once more and she had to bite down – hard – on her lip to stop from moaning. "But that does not mean I want, nor invite, your counsel."

How could she feel such heat and want when he was cutting her down so mercilessly?

"But Addan valued…"

"Do not speak to me of my brother!" The words were fierce and she startled, surprised by his anger but also by the depth of his hurt. She felt it ravaging him and she understood. "Not while we are doing this." He stared at her as he thrust inside her and her chest exploded with feelings.

Because he was right and yet none of this felt wrong,

none of it felt like a betrayal of the man they'd both loved and lost.

"I have no interest in competing with him," he said, bringing his mouth to hers, his mouth warm against her own, his tongue sliding inside, clashing with hers. He moved faster and deeper, his arousal possessing every single part of her, tormenting her with the perfection of his possession.

She arched her back, needing more, wanting all of him, and yet he held himself still, pushing up on his elbows to see her once more.

"You are my wife." The words rang through the room, and they made no sense and complete sense all at once.

"Yes. And I want that to be more than just sex."

His eyes locked to hers and then he rolled them easily, pulling her to his chest, holding her hips as he thrust into her, his eyes fixated on her breasts as she moved up and down his length.

"You cannot change what we are, *sharafaha*," he said, and she blotted the words out, because she was riding a wave that demanded all her attention, all her focus. She dug her nails into his shoulders, bringing her body down against his, so her sensitive nipples scraped against his hair-roughened chest.

"You think?"

And she moved now, her own body lifting faster, taking him deeper, so that when she exploded it was with Malik in her grip, Malik falling apart with her, his hoarse cry spilling into the room as his body emptied into hers.

She lay on top of him, spent, exhausted and strangely sad, despite the incredible euphoria she'd just experienced.

Malik held her for a moment, their breath equally frantic and heavy, and then he rolled her onto her back, pushing himself up onto his elbow to look down at her.

"I think we married under duress," he said quietly,

roaming her face with his indolent gaze. "And that our relationship is not what yours was with Addan."

"But it can be more than this –,"

He pressed a finger to her lips, silencing her.

"It will never be more than sex." The words were fired with intent and determination. "I have no interest in becoming your friend and confidante, of pretending to be what Addan was to you. Do not make the mistake of imagining you can replace my brother so easily."

His words were like bullets against her heart and a burst of anger jackknifed out of her chest. She was surprised by his callousness, angered by the way he spoke of her relationship and Addan.

"Don't you think I know that?" She sat up, her fury contained in every line of her body. "Don't you think I've always known that? Where he was a man of honour and kindness, gentle and thoughtful, compassionate and cerebral, you are the barbarian equivalent, all brawn and no Goddamned heart! You will never be even a tenth of the man he was. I didn't ask for any of this and I'm doing my level best to be everything this country needs. And all I'm asking in exchange is respect and some common decency."

She glared at him angrily, hurt making her lash out. "I've hated you for as long as I've known you but for Addan, I concealed that. And now we're married and I want to do what I've been trained for – I want to be a part of this country."

He was very still, not reacting to her tirade, not showing – at first – that he'd even heard her words.

"Then you must get pregnant and give my country an heir. As soon as we have our royal bloodline assured, you can go back to hating me from the other side of the palace. And believe me when I say that day can't come soon enough."

HE ONLY SLEPT AN HOUR, and it was a fitful sleep. His dreams were broken. Full of the desert and the eagles he travelled with, his brother and their last trip together.

And he dreamt of his wife. Her soft, naked body, pliable and sweet and so hungry for him. So hungry she couldn't resist him even when she loved Addan, when she wished he had lived and she was married to him now.

He saw her earnest expression, asking him about the desert tribes, and he felt that same swell of resentment he'd felt that afternoon.

He heard the words she'd thrown at him.

Where he was a man of honour and kindness, gentle and thoughtful, compassionate and cerebral, you are the barbarian equivalent, all brawn and no Goddamned heart! You will never be even a tenth of the man he was.

Her words drummed through his soul with a violence that surprised him. Not the thoughts – they were no surprise. But his reaction to them! Hearing someone speak your misgivings aloud, having someone confirm for you what you know to be the absolute truth – it sat inside him like a rock and a blade, so that, after an hour of fitful tossing and turning he gave up on sleep, dressed, and went to his office to brood and be generally discontent.

Only there, in what he had once considered his sanctuary, her words hounded him. He heard them butting against the ancient tapestries, flying at him from all directions, her manner in issuing them so infuriatingly superior.

But it wasn't that which had got under his skin.

It was her heartbreak.

The stoicism with which she tried to hide it – and failed. It was the way she invoked Addan so easily, as though he were still living, as though in talking to Malik she could keep him alive.

It was her grief.

A grief he understood, for it was one he shared.

In this, they were united. In this, they were alike.

But only this.

He looked down at his skin and an image came to him of her own, pressed against it, so pale and fair – the perfect opposite.

The first time he saw Sophia, she'd been just a girl. A tiny little sprite with blonde hair that fell all the way down her back, skinny with enormous blue eyes, half the size of her face it had seemed. Malik had been twelve, Sophia eight, and she had eyes only for Addan.

He came into the grand hall to find them bent over an ancient book, her hair falling like a curtain, sunlight streaming in through the window overhead, and he'd stood, frozen in the doorframe. All he could do was stare at this creature, who looked almost like a desert fairy brought to life- the same colour as the sands beyond the palace, and just as mysterious.

Addan whispered something and she laughed, her voice peeling towards him, and he instantly saw another little girl, a girl who'd been lost- like a fair ghost. She lifted her head to say something to Addan and Malik had instinctively shifted into the shadows, wanting to look and not yet be seen.

Her voice was too low to catch but it was obvious she was trying to speak in Abu Fayan, though her accent was dreadful.

Addan simply nodded encouragingly and answered in English.

She smiled, her cheeks glowing pink, and Malik felt something unpleasant and cross unfurl in his gut.

He left without introducing himself.

Later in her visit, he'd met her quite by accident. She'd been running through the marble corridors that were a feature of the East wing and he'd stepped out of the gym, having been playing tennis, and they'd collided.

She'd skidded across the corridor, bumping into an ancient statue and almost setting it flying.

He'd steadied it and crouched down to her at the same time. "You should not be running in here!" His voice had been furious, even to his own ears. He reminded himself of his uncle – how often had he been chastised for doing exactly that?

Her lower lip jutted out and for a second he thought she might cry. Then, she'd scrambled to her feet and slammed her hands onto her hips, glaring at him.

"Yeah, well, you should wear a cowbell or something, if you're going to sneak around like that."

"I was simply exiting a room and did not expect a little tornado to burst through me."

"I'm not a tornado," she snapped. "And I'm playing tag. Running is kind of the point."

"Well take your game somewhere more sensible. Perhaps the courtyard?"

She pouted. "It's hot out there."

"Yes. This is a hot country. What's your point?"

She'd glared at him and then laughed. "He was right about you. You can be a real grump."

She had skipped away without waiting to see the look on his face.

CHAPTER 6

TWO DAYS PASSED AND she refused to go to him. She refused to seek him out. She refused to even let him know she was thinking of him.

Her temper didn't abate.

How dare he act as though her only function within this marriage was to incubate a royal heir? She'd been chosen for this role by his father, and groomed for it almost since birth. She had studied this country, its politics, its history, almost her whole life. To be told she had no counsel to offer by its ruler – her own husband! – stung.

"You don't think the necklace is too much?" she murmured thoughtfully, thinking longingly of the simple one Addan had given her that she preferred for all occasions, while staring at her reflection in the mirror as one of her servants clipped the diamond choker in place.

"It goes with the tiara," the servant said, bowing low and stepping backwards.

Sophia's eyes lifted to the delicate diamond crown that had been placed on her head. Despite its lace-like construction, it was heavy – filled with gems and cast of platinum gold – but her hair had been braided through it, weaving in and out of the bottom so that it was at one with her head. And yes, the servant was right. The choker was indeed a perfect match.

Her eyes shifted to the girl in the reflection. Since her marriage, this young woman had been attending to her every day. "What is your name?"

"Awan, your highness."

"Awan," Sophia smiled, barely recognizing her own image in the mirror. The dress was so formal, so beautiful. She looked every bit the princess she now was – the princess she'd been groomed to become, almost her whole life. "How old are you?"

"Nineteen, madam."

Sophia's smile was wistful. They were close in age but very different in terms of cares and responsibility.

"Have you worked at the palace long?"

"Yes, your highness." Awan bowed. "I was hired two years ago."

Sophia smiled. "And what did you do before this?"

"I was training for this," she said earnestly. "To be one of your maids."

The synchronicity of that wasn't lost on Sophia. "So we've both been in training a long time."

"Madam?"

"Never mind." Sophia straightened, running her hands down the gown she wore. A royal blue with a sheen through the fabric, it showed off the creamy luminescence of her skin and complimented the sparkling blue of her eyes.

"His Highness is already at the car," Awan said. "And awaits your arrival."

Sophia lifted a brow. "I guess that's a polite way of telling me to move my butt."

Awan hid her smile – just.

. . .

HE WAS WAITING by the car and the second she saw him, her step faltered. She slowed, giving herself the maximum time possible to prepare for this, to prepare for being in his orbit again. Her insides looped in on one another. Her body swooped and roared.

His royal highness, Sheikh Malik bin Hazari was standing beside the limousine, wearing the traditional white robes of his people, his expression stern, his face mesmerizing with its harsh angles and planes and determined, sculpted lips. His eyes were constant, locked to her face. Her stomach looped and rolled as she got closer to him until, finally, at the car, she breathed in and the masculine fragrance that was so uniquely her husband infiltrated her blood and her senses, fairly bowling Sophia over.

"Malik," she murmured, holding his gaze even when the force of desire she felt for him threatened to fell her at the knees.

"*Sharafaha*," he murmured, dropping his head closer to hers for a moment, so she thought he might kiss her.

He didn't. Instead, his eyes stared into hers, as though just by looking at her he could understand her, as though he could read everything she was feeling and thinking. Then, he straightened, his own expression inscrutable.

Disappointment sledged against her as he took a backwards step and gestured towards the limousine.

"After you."

"Thank you." She slid into the vehicle, her pulse hammering, her mind racing.

She'd been to parliament twice before. Once with Addan, to explore the ancient tunnels that ran beneath the building, tunnels that were built at the turn of the first millennia, to offer protection for the people of this city, when attacks were commonplace. And once, to sign the vows of marriage, to bind herself to this country and its Sheikh for all time.

Tonight would be her first time visiting as a royal.

How different she'd felt on her previous visit! Excited and overjoyed, on the brink of stepping into her new life, of formalizing this marriage she'd anticipated for so long. The world had seemed so simple, her purpose so clear. And now?

It was all as clear as river mud.

"It is just a dinner party," his deeply-intoned words jolted her out of her reverie, as the car pulled away from the palace.

She turned to face him, her eyes round in her pretty face. "A cocktail party, I thought."

"Yes." He frowned, his eyes scanning her features, looking at her with the same intensity as moments earlier – as though he could decode her if only he stared long enough.

Sophia had no interest in being decoded, though.

She sat back against the seat and turned to look out of her own window.

After several minutes had passed, he spoke again. "You are annoyed at me."

She wiped an imaginary piece of lint from her dress, keeping her expression carefully muted of any emotion. She wasn't annoyed. She was livid and cross, angry and hurt. She was a thousand things, all bottled up inside of her. She remembered the way they'd parted, two nights earlier.

It will never be more than sex.

What had she expected? Passionate declarations of love? No. Nothing so juvenile. Only she'd entered this marriage presuming they could build on something, that they would find a way to have a real relationship. It had never occurred to Sophia that sex alone was all Malik would offer, nor that it would be all he sought from her.

With a steely gaze and a coldness to her tone, she arched a

brow, turning her vibrant blue eyes to him with obvious derision. "Do you care if I am?"

Silence laced around them, thudding in the car, throbbing with words not spoken and questions not asked. "Yes."

Sophia's heart pounded against her ribs, his admission not at all what she'd expected.

"Surprisingly," he tacked on, showing himself to be aware of how little sense that made.

"I *am* surprised," she said, earning a tight grimace from him.

"A long time ago, I promised Addan I would be kind to you," he said, after a moment. Sophia's heart lurched, memories of her friend making her chest hurt. "It occurs to me I have broken that promise."

"Addan wanted us to be friends," she said softly, remembering his entreaties with a small shake of her head, the past like quicksand that would swallow her in its memories if she weren't careful. "He could never understand why we…"

"Could not stand one another?"

She murmured her agreement. "Addan liked to think everyone could find common ground."

"And what do you think, Sophia?"

She observed him through narrowed eyes and then shrugged her slender shoulders, as though none of this mattered. "I think you are determined not to like me, not even a little bit. Beyond that, what does common ground matter?"

He was quiet and watchful for several seconds before responding. "What do you base this opinion on?"

Her laugh was a short, sharp sound. "Don't insult my intelligence by trying to deny it."

"I'm not denying it," he said quietly.

"Good. I know how you feel about me. I know how you felt about me as Addan's fiancé. You could never understand the reason for our betrothal. You thought me undeserving of him and undeserving of this role, and now you're stuck with me." She crossed her arms over her chest, watching him through shuttered eyes.

"It would appear so," he drawled, but there was ice in the statement.

"Can't you see that you're the only person fighting this?"

"I married you," he said firmly. "We are doing what we can to provide this country with an heir. How exactly am I fighting this?"

"You're boxing me up, keeping me in one tiny compartment of your life…"

"We have discussed this. Our marriage requires that we –,"

"Yes, yes, I know," she interrupted crossly. "An heir. I get it. But Addan wanted me to be his equal in every way. That's what I'm trained for, and I'm ready for that, Malik."

The engine was cut. In moments, the door would be opened.

"You don't care for me like Addan did. Fine. What he and I shared was completely different. With Addan and me there was such a meeting of the minds, we were so well-suited…"

Malik's features tightened.

"Get to know me better, and you'll see why Addan trusted me."

"I know you."

A shiver ran down her spine then – not of fear but of comprehension, because nothing about Malik's statement rang false. He looked to her and she felt something lock into place, because he *did* know her. He didn't like her, necessarily, but there was some kind of innate understanding between them, something that defied logic and sense. Perhaps it was their connection through Addan?

"And I know what you were to Addan, and how much he

adored you. Do you think a single minute of this damned marriage passes without me remembering how he loved you?"

The window beyond Malik darkened – a sign that a guard was on the other side, poised to open the door, and the Sheikh reached for the frame and pressed the lock button down.

It was deftly done – for they were in privacy, with the windows shielded from the view of the crowds.

When he turned to face her, there was a tightness about his features, a look of absolute iron-like determination.

"Do you think a single minute of this marriage passes without me remembering that you were his fiancé?" The words were tortured, but his gaze locked to hers with clarity.

He bent forward and found the hem of her skirt, lifting it, bringing it higher up her body, his hand gliding over her calves, her knee, her thighs before brushing against her womanhood through the silk of her underwear.

She gasped and bit back a moan at his touch, her body breaking out with a feverish need. "But do not forget, *Sharafaha,* I am the only man who can make you feel like this." And he slid a finger inside her moist core, swirling it around her tight, aching muscles and she bit down on her lip, lifting a hand to his robes and curving her fingers in the fabric there.

"You had his heart, I have no doubt," he said, coldly, cynically, with very little emotion. "But your body is all mine, Sophia. Don't forget that."

IT HAD all happened so quickly. One minute he was tormenting her with desire, pleasuring her in a way that made her soul sing, and the next, when she was frustratingly close to orgasm he pulled away, his expression constrained.

"Come to my room tonight, Sheikha."

And he turned away, giving her a moment to straighten her skirt before knocking on the window and inviting the guard to open the doors.

Photographers were everywhere, and the adoring public here to catch a glimpse of their royal couple, out in droves. Thousands strong, lined on both sides of the street.

Sophia had walked the lines like an automaton, her knees shaking, her stomach in knots, her every thought on what had just happened.

Come to my room tonight, Sheikha.

Her stomach looped at the very idea that within hours they would be back at the palace and she could be in his arms once more, finishing what he'd just started.

And not finished, Sophia reminded herself forcefully, her lips compressing to form a grim line in her face. How dare he stir her up like that after two days of *nothing* and leave her without the big bang? She might be new to the whole sex thing but that smacked of bad etiquette.

She lifted her head, incensed, and across the street, where he was speaking with someone in the crowd, he turned to her at the same time. Their eyes met and Sophia would have sworn lightning struck from him to her. Localized and intense, it seared her nerve endings, but she couldn't back away. She stared at him and he at her and then someone asked her a question, a child handed her a teddy bear, and she was jolted back to the present.

But her nerve endings were firing and her pulse was racing. She was humming with anticipation.

She needed ... what?

She needed *him*.

The realization slammed against her sides and she hated it. She hated that for all his failings, all his faults, she *needed* this man with a visceral, undeniable ache.

It would have been so much easier if she'd married Addan. Darling Addan, who had been so kind and good, and uncomplicated; who had loved her like a sister. But that love had been just what Sophia had craved all her life. Dependable, steady, safe, not-going-anywhere love.

But he was gone. Nothing was safe, nothing was foolproof, least of all the future.

She forced a smile to her face as she moved down the line until she'd circled back and Malik was waiting for her at the bottom of the stairs that led to parliament. It was a balmy evening, the sky tinged with purple and gold, and a red carpet was running down the steps all the way to the street. Candles were lit on the front of the building, enormous and flickering in the fading light.

At her side, he put a hand in the small of her back and shocks of desire arrowed through her veins, all the way to a heart that was beating far too fast.

She resisted the impulse to look at him, keeping a firm smile pinned to her face, lifting a hand and waving at their people. Huge signs were waving in the evening air, some with her photograph, others with her name. Whatever her husband might think of her suitability to be Sheikha, it was not – apparently – a sentiment the population of Abu Faya shared.

"I THINK education is a cornerstone of any civilized society." The Sheikha's voice carried to him even though she was across the room, and he was in the middle of his own conversation. It was as though she had the ability to tunnel right down inside of him, to speak to something deep in his being.

He lifted his head, pinpointing her with his gaze, curious

as to who she was speaking to – curious and alive with a possessive heat he hadn't felt in a long time.

Ali Burkhan, a thirty-something investor in the private education sector, and a friend of Malik's from when they were teenagers.

Ali smiled. "Indeed."

"Affordable, and accessible education," she added meaningfully.

He laughed. "Didn't we speak about this on the yacht last summer," Ali drawled, leaning a little closer, so that something inside Malik fired. He didn't catch the rest of what Ali was saying and now he wished to be nearer to his wife and friend, to be a part of their conversation.

"Excuse me." He nodded curtly towards the couple he'd been exchanging pleasantries with. The royal couple had been at this affair for three hours. Parliament had officially welcomed his wife, and now he wanted to have her all to himself again.

"And nothing in your policies has changed," she was murmuring, smiling, an easy, natural smile that was remarkable for two reasons. Her smile was one of the most beautiful things Malik had ever seen. And looking at it now, Malik realised she'd never smiled like that for him.

It was no surprise. They were generally arguing with one another, and yet, he realised now how often she'd smiled and laughed with his brother. How easily she smiled now.

His stomach tightened but he didn't approach them. He hovered just outside of their range, looking without interrupting.

"Don't think I haven't noticed that," she added for good measure, the lightness to her tone drawing him in, warming him.

"Have you been checking up on me?"

"Well, your website at least," she winked, and Ali laughed

– Malik, on the other hand, was not amused. He knew enough of his wife's easy nature to know she wasn't flirting. Charm came easily to her – she did it without thinking, reflexively. But that didn't lessen the impact it had on Malik.

Suddenly, as though lightning had pierced his soul, splitting him clear in two, he remembered how close Sophia had come to marrying another man. How he had been so close to living his whole life like this – looking at her from the outside, watching her smile and laugh, with no right to touch her, to kiss her, to hold her, to make her cry his name out.

And a dark, angry guilt churned through him, because his own brother's death was the only reason they were married. Had Addan lived, she would be his by now, perhaps rounded with his child in her belly.

Frustration gnawed at his insides. She was his wife – it was done. Finished. No matter what *should* have been her life, they'd found themselves here.

"I think you'll find, your highness, that we've widened our selection criteria *and* dropped the age of applicants."

"I *did* notice that," she conceded.

"And it is a step in the right direction, yes?"

She tilted her head to the side, feigning deep-thought. "I suppose so," she murmured, a dimple in her cheek flashing when she grinned at Ali. "But don't think this lets you off the hook. I'll be watching you."

Ali dipped his head forward in a bow. "And I hope to earn your approval."

Malik stepped closer and Sophia lifted her head, a smile still on her face when she looked at him.

"It is time to leave."

Her smile disappeared completely.

"Mal," Ali extended his hand and Malik shook it. Ali was one of the few people who referred to him so casually – and it didn't occur to Malik to mind. "How's it going?"

"Fine." He nodded in curt acknowledgment.

"Her highness here was just trying to guilt me into opening up my scholarship program one-hundred-fold."

"And I've explained why," she turned back to Ali, smiling once more, though with an air of constraint now. "You have no idea what potential you are limiting by not granting scholarships to intelligent, gifted, but financially impoverished students. What if the person who will cure cancer for good is living in one of the slums to the east?"

"Well, the slums, majesties, rather fall into your domain," he pointed out archly.

Malik shifted his weight from one foot to the other. "It isn't an easy problem to address."

"I am only teasing your wife, Mal," Ali grinned, and Malik was impatient now for this to be at an end.

He lifted his hand to Sophia's back and felt her tremble in response, and he understood. Heat blazed between them, just as it had in the limousine earlier that evening, just as it always did. Her eyes lifted to his and despite the easy exchange she'd just shared with Ali, there was tension in her expression now. Tension that he understood, because he felt the same.

"Are you ready to leave, your highness?" He murmured, running his fingers over her spine, feeling each ridge, each bump, each little intake of breath. The rest of the world dropped away. Ali was no longer there, nor were the other members of parliament.

She nodded wordlessly, her eyes locked to his, and smiled. A tight smile, forced, nothing like the easy expression she'd offered Ali a moment earlier.

"Then let us leave. Excuse us, friend," he murmured to Ali, steering Sophia away from the crowds, his expression one that didn't invite interruption. The doors were opened for them by servants and they moved down the stairs. People were waiting, and they cheered as Sophia and Malik emerged. She smiled, lifted a hand a little to wave, but otherwise stayed right where she was, her body molded to his side, so close he could feel her breathing.

And he kept his hand clamped around her waist, glad she was at his side, but knowing he'd be gladder still when she was in his bed.

CHAPTER 7

"HOW DO YOU KNOW Ali?"

They'd left parliament at least ten minutes earlier and neither of them had spoken. Sophia's heart was in her throat, desire hot and desperate between her legs. She blinked across at her husband, his question unexpected. All she could do was hold her breath and wait – wait to be back in the privacy of the palace and in his arms.

"Through Addan," she said simply.

But it wasn't simple. At least, not for Malik. "You mentioned last summer?"

"We spent a week on a yacht with him and some other friends," she said, shaking her head. "Only a few months before…"

His eyes swept her face thoughtfully. "You and Addan travelled together, and still your relationship never became sexual?"

Heat filled her cheeks. "No."

"How did he explain that? You had your own rooms, I presume, on this yacht?"

"Addan didn't explain anything," she said, stiffly, defensively, when she knew she didn't need to defend Addan to his own brother. She sighed, turning to look out of the window. "I think it was just accepted amongst our friends that we were waiting until we were married."

The words hung awkwardly between them.

"That's absurd."

"Why?"

"Because it's the twenty first century and you're two consenting adults…"

"Yeah, well, I think it's romantic," she said quietly, not willing to hear anything approaching criticism of Addan. "And are you so very different? Would you not have expected your wife to be some innocent virgin?" Her cynicism was evident in the tone of her voice.

"Until the night my brother died, I had no intentions of marrying anyone."

She frowned. "Why?"

He frowned. "Why would I?"

"I… because it's what you do? Because it's… family?"

"We're all born alone, Sophia. We die alone. Why commit myself to someone for the rest of my life when I can do what I want? I like freedom. I like… independence."

Something fogged in Sophia's mind. A long-ago conversation with Addan.

"He scares me." She whispered, beneath the sheets, the torch they'd brought with them casting shadows around them.

"Who, Malik?"

"Yes! He's so… big and he never smiles."

"People who feel deepest are often the slowest to open up. He doesn't smile – that doesn't mean he doesn't care. And it certainly doesn't mean you should be afraid of him. My brother is a good man, Sophia. A better man than I am, and he would have made a far better Sheikh too, except in one vital way."

"What's that?" She'd whispered, even though they were alone.

"He will never do what he's told – and sometimes, as King, you have to."

She'd been thirteen. The conversation was so clear that for a moment she felt like she was slipping down a slope, with nothing to grab onto.

"How come you married me?" She asked, her heart skidding to a stop in her chest.

Malik stiffened beside her. "Because I inherited the throne."

"And me," she nodded, pushing that aside. "But you didn't want this."

"No." He spat the word with such vehemence she was surprised it didn't hurt more.

"Marriage to anyone? Or me, in particular?"

He turned to look at her, his dark eyes swirling with emotions she couldn't comprehend. "You were my brother's fiancé," he said, after a long pause. "He loved you to the ends of the earth. How could I ever want this?"

Her stomach squeezed. They'd been married a little over a fortnight and the idea of him not wanting her, made her feel as though her lungs were filling with sand. She bit down on her lower lip and looked forward.

"I didn't want to marry anyone," he said, after a moment, "But my brother's death put the Kingdom in a dangerous position. Not having another living heir means the throne would pass, upon my death, to a distant cousin with ties to questionable organisations. The order of succession must be protected." A muscle jerked in his jaw. "And you were here, legally mine, whether I wanted that or not."

Pain shimmied inside of her. Desire, hot between her legs, was a traitor now, a sensation she didn't want, something she didn't relish. She drew in a gulp of air; it barely reached her lungs.

"I'm sorry you have to endure this, then," she said coldly, looking away from him.

She heard his exhalation. "It is *you* who has to endure this. Marriage to a man you didn't choose, this should never have been your fate."

"I did choose this," she said simply. "I chose all of this."

They didn't speak the rest of the way to the palace.

AT THE ENTRANCE to the family suites, he put a hand in her back, guiding her towards his room. She didn't resist, and he was glad. There'd been a part of him that thought, despite the sexual heat buzzing between them, their conversation in the car might have killed her need for him.

It hadn't.

He pushed his door open and as soon as they were inside, her hands found his chest, her fingers splayed wide as she pushed herself up onto the tips of her toes and kissed him.

It was a kiss of fire and anger, dark emotions making her lips mash his, her tongue move furiously. And he understood.

This was all darkness between them. No wonder she didn't smile for him.

Even their passion was born of a dark place. It was possessive and resented.

Neither of them wanted to feel this, and yet they did – and it was overwhelming.

He swore in his own language, untying his robes with one hand, fumbling a little as he slipped them from his body, pushing out of his briefs at the same time so he was naked, and desperate to see her naked too. But he was more desperate for her. He needed her in a way that was like fire in his gut.

He grabbed her hips and lifted her, pushing at the layers of her skirt, finding the briefs he'd slipped aside so easily earlier that night.

"Hold this," He grunted, pushing the layers of skirt into her hand. She took them from him and now he lifted her and kissed her, pushing her back against the cold, hard wall behind him. He spread her legs, his strength great, her body slender. He wrapped her legs around his waist, his eyes watching hers as he nudged the tip of his arousal at her sex.

"Do you want me?" He demanded, his eyes latched to hers.

She laughed, but it was a tortured, rasping sound. "What do you think?"

"I want you to scream my name when you come," he dropped his mouth to her throat, nipping her flesh there, smiling when she groaned. He pushed his erection forward slightly, and she cried out, 'yes', over and over, her nails digging into his shoulders.

"Yes, what?" He pulled back.

"Please," she groaned, digging her ankles into the small of his back in an attempt to pull him deeper.

"Beg me," he said simply.

"Why?"

Because you were my brother's in every way except this. Because I alone make you feel this. Because I want you to admit that in this way, we own each other.

"Because I say so."

She bit down on her lip and rolled her hips, her arousal at fever pitch.

He could feel her trembling and knew her release would be swift and powerful. He wanted to give her that, he wanted to make her come hard and fast and then he wanted to tease and torment her body all night long, bringing her to the point of explosion again and again until finally letting her fall apart.

"You're such a bastard," she groaned.

"A bastard you want inside you."

She rolled her hips again. "Yes. Damn it, yes. Please, Malik, please."

His chest burst with an explosion of relief and he thrust into her, so hard and fast that he felt some of his own seed drop into her. With the utmost control, he steadied himself, holding his own pleasure at bay as he thrust into her again and again, watching as she became incoherent with desire, vowing they would never spend another night apart.

"You are moving to my room," he grunted, as she called his name, finally, over and over, and he thought he'd never heard anything so sexy. "This is where you belong."

She screamed when she came, pleasure pulling her apart at the seams, her heels digging into his back, her nails scratching his flesh, her teeth clamping down on his shoulder. She was wracked with heavy breathing, the intensity of their coming together exploding around them.

He held her while her breath stilled, he felt the moment passion overtook resentment and he understood why. He'd never made a woman beg for him – though plenty had.

He'd never used sex as a carrot to entice a woman to do what he wanted. He'd never withheld pleasure as a means to compel someone to carry out his wishes.

He would have been ashamed, except it had felt so damned good.

She pulled away from him, lifting her head, looking over his shoulder, her expression showing she was at war with herself. There was a wariness to her he didn't like seeing. A sense of uncertainty that he wanted to erase.

"Why did you do that?"

He rolled his hips and she jerked, her eyes slashing to his, heavy with desire and sparking with resentment.

He sighed, lifting her away from the wall without breaking their connection.

"I'm serious, Malik…"

Now, when she said his name, it was thick with hurt and that did something inside him. He expelled a breath, kissing her gently as he laid her down on the bed. "I like to know you are thinking of me when we do this," he said simply.

Her eyes flew wide and resentment gave way to compassion – which he hated. He didn't want that. But she was giving it to him anyway, pushing up on her elbows and kissing him, her tongue dueling with his, her hands tangling in his hair.

"Who else would I be thinking of?"

He didn't answer. He didn't need to. The ghost of Addan was alive enough for both of them to perceive him.

There was no point speaking his name.

SHE'D GO SOON. When her eyes were a little less heavy. And her arms less exhausted. And her… she fell asleep and woke with a start sometime before dawn, disoriented and starving.

It was still dark, but the air had changed. The cool of the evening was being drawn out, and heat was replacing it, thick and stultifying. She moved slightly and came up against something hard and warm.

Her body stilled. She spun in bed and it all came crashing back to her.

She'd fallen asleep in his bed.

And no wonder.

Her pulse began to throb inside of her as memories surged. Memories of the way they'd made love so hard and fast against the wall like two jungle animals. Of the way he'd made her beg for him, and how furious she'd been.

And then, his admission – the reasons it mattered to him. And her heart had burst. She'd felt… she'd felt sympathy and something far more dangerous. Something unwanted and unpleasant.

She'd wanted to hug him.

She'd wanted to tell him she'd never needed another person in the way she did him. That the depth of her physical desire was enough to make her want to walk to the ends of the earth. That she would do just about anything he asked of her, if it meant more of this.

That she was his very willing sex slave, and she wasn't even sure she cared. But there was so much danger in even admitting that to herself; she couldn't admit that to Malik. Not yet. He was too much. Too powerful and closed off to her. She couldn't be vulnerable to him – not more than she already was.

They'd had sex, and then, he'd tormented her body in the best possible way for hours, driving her to the point of oblivion, his mouth moving over her most sensitive nerve endings, teasing her, delighting her, his hands controlling her body, showing him to be a maestro of her in every way.

It had been somewhere near three when she'd exploded, and he with her, their hoarse cries mingling, the sound of release ricocheting around the room. And she'd intended to get up and leave almost immediately afterwards, but he'd clamped an arm around her waist and fallen asleep, and it had felt so good just being there, her body had been weak and exhausted.

But daylight was coming and everything looked different now.

She shifted in the bed a little, moving away from him, watching him, making sure he stayed sleeping. She pushed her feet out and stood, swallowing as she turned away from him. The dress she'd worn the night before had been left on the floor; it was dreadfully crushed, but that wouldn't matter. She pulled it up silently, dragging her hair over one shoulder and checking her appearance in a small mirror as she approached the door.

Her heart burst up a gear because she looked like exactly what she was: a woman who had been thoroughly made love to all night. Her eyes had silver grey circles beneath them, her lips were dark and heavy, her skin had stubble rash across it.

"Going somewhere, Cinderella?"

She startled, spinning around to find her husband watching her with indolent speculation, the sheet discarded so she could see for herself that last night's release hadn't abated his desire for her one bit.

She swallowed, staring at his arousal, feeling a flood of desire thick within her abdomen.

"Come back to bed."

It was a command. That alone made her want to defy it.

"Please."

And then he did something like that. She weakened, staying where she was but smiling a little.

"Playing hard to get?" He prompted, standing in one lithe movement, striding across to her, his powerful body mesmerizing for its strength and vitality.

"I'm not playing anything, Malik," she murmured softly. "I didn't mean to wake you."

He made a tsking noise of disapproval. "And what if I want you to wake me?"

He reached for her hand, his eyes slightly mocking as they held hers. "What if I want you to do this?" He curved her hands over his length and she made a groaning noise as she felt his strength throb in her palm.

He brought his mouth closer to hers, brushing his lips over hers. "Stay here."

Of its own accord, her hand moved up his length, her fingertips brushing over his tip. He made a noise deep in his throat of pleasure, and power exploded inside of her.

She had done that. She'd made him feel that. She moved her hand down to the base of his arousal and then up again, squeezing a little and he tilted his head back, exhaling on a hiss as he stared at the ceiling, before sweeping his eyes shut.

And suddenly, she wanted to feel all-powerful, even more than this.

"I was a virgin before our wedding night," she said simply, and he jerked his head down, looking at her. "And now we've slept together. But I don't know how to do… anything else."

Holding his gaze, she dropped to her knees, her eyes huge in her face. "Will you tell me?" She darted her tongue out and ran it over his tip, a thrill of strength bursting through her as she felt him tremble.

"Sophia," he moved a little, stepping back slightly, but she shuffled forward, her hands curling around the base of his arousal, holding him where he was.

"And I want you to say my name," she warned, her eyes sparking with his, as she opened her mouth wide enough to take his tip into her moistness.

He swore, his body rigid.

She took him deeper, slowly, letting herself get used to this new feeling, to this different kind of invasion. She moved her mouth up and down his length, challenging herself with how deep she could take him each time, until finally his tip hitched against the back of her throat and he groaned low and harsh.

His fingers found her hair, curling in its blonde lengths, the pressure gentle but incredibly arousing. She rolled her hips, desire sparking inside of her as she tasted a drop of his come in her mouth.

He swore, the sound so intensely hot, and then his hands were beneath her arms, lifting her, pulling her away from him, and he cradled her against his chest as he carried her back to bed.

"This damned dress," he grunted, pushing the skirts up around her waist, his eyes showing impatience that made her laugh, despite her own needs being just as desperate.

"I didn't want to go naked through the corridors," she pointed out, but then his hands pushed her legs apart, wide and strong, and he thrust into her, so speech and thought became utterly impossible as pleasure seared her.

She arched her back, and he made a noise of impatience, one hand lifting to the top of her dress and pulling it. The dress tore.

She barely noticed. His hand cupped her breasts and then his mouth came down on her nipple, his tongue lashing her in time with each thrust, and then his teeth clamping on the engorged flesh until she was moaning his name over and over – no need to be asked this time.

"Malik," she arched her back, pushing her hips up, taking him deeper and he drove into her as he moved his mouth to her other breast and she writhed beneath him, lost to this utterly and completely. "I need…"

"I know," he reached up, his fingers curling into her hair, holding her head still as he took completely possession of her body and finally, she exploded, a burst of stars on the outside of her mind as pleasure contorted her being.

She closed her eyes, her body flooded with sensations, her mind unable to think of anything outside of this. She lay beneath him, his weight a pleasure, his closeness a godsend, and she simply felt.

She felt everything.

And then, he shifted out of her, moving to his side of the bed. "Go back to sleep, *sharafaha.* It is still dark out."

She frowned, following his gaze to the window. It was dark, but there was a glow on the very edges of the horizon. Soon, morning would come, and there'd be light again, because light always followed the dark.

CHAPTER 8

S HE WOKE TO THE ringing of the phone and an empty bed. Pushing up, squinting, Sophia focused her gaze on the clock across the room. It was still early. Seven something.

She blinked, turning to the phone, reaching for the receiver on autopilot.

"Yeah, hello?"

Rapid fire Abu Fayan greeted her. "His highness is required immediately. Please ask him to come to the State rooms in the East wing."

She frowned as the line went dead, replacing the receiver and pushing out of bed in one movement. She padded across the room, naked, and peered into the lounge area of the suite. Empty.

The bathroom was also empty. The kitchen likewise.

With a frown, she moved towards the balcony and it was here that she saw him.

Naked from the waist up, wearing only a pair of black briefs that showed his powerful trunk-like legs, tapered waist and muscular shoulders, her brow beaded with fine perspiration.

Why did she love his hair so much? He seemed to habitually pull it up into a very messy bun, himself, undoubtedly for comfort. But there was something so hot about that, about the way it sat there all dark and straining against confinement.

He turned, his eyes latching to hers, and Sophia's breath snagged in her throat at the fact he'd caught her unashamedly staring.

"You're awake."

She nodded, her throat thick.

"I thought you might sleep all day."

"No." She shook her head. "The phone rang."

His eyes narrowed. "I apologise. I told my assistant I was not to be disturbed."

"It sounded important. You're wanted in the State room of the East wing immediately."

His expression tightened. "Damn it."

"What?""

"Laith. It doesn't matter. It's something I have to deal with."

But the name was familiar to Sophia. "The *Jakari*?"

He nodded dismissively. "Yes."

"What is it?"

"I don't know any more than you do. I must go." He moved past her but then, thought better of it, turning back to her. "I'll come and see you before I leave."

"You think you'll have to go out into the desert again?"

His lips compressed. "Yes, *sharafaha*, I think I will have to go to him and sort this out in person."

She didn't say what she was thinking. There was no sense in having a battle with him until they both knew what he was dealing with. But as soon as he left, she gathered her torn dress to her body and moved back to her own room.

She showered and changed at speed, choosing loose linen

pants and a flowy shirt. Her hair she scraped back into a low pony-tail before throwing some clothes and toiletries into a simple backpack and returning with speed to his suite.

It was empty.

She made a coffee, sipping it, trying to calm the kaleido-scope of butterflies that was battering her tummy.

It was almost an hour before he returned – or, three coffees and a sticky almond biscuit that tasted like sunshine and smiles.

He was distracted when he entered, his expression tense, and he was flanked by two ministerial staff and two servants, all dressed in the traditional white robes of Abu Faya. It was strange that, even when dressed in similar clothes, Malik looked so different.

So primeval and elemental.

Her stomach swooped as his eyes dropped to the bag at her feet then lifted to her face, clashing with hers again.

"Leave us." He spoke to his staff without addressing them. It mattered not. They bowed low and exited through the wide doorway, pulling it closed behind them.

Before he could speak, she straightened, her eyes holding a challenge. "You're going into the desert? To the *Jakari*?"

If it was possible, his expression tightened. Slowly, he nodded. "I'll be away a week or so."

"That's fine. I'm coming with you."

He didn't visibly react. "Your place is here."

"No," she shook her head. "My place is at your side, remember? We're married. I'm Sheikha. I've spent a long time training to be a Queen to your people. I don't intend to have all that education go to waste."

"Reading about ancient feuds and living amongst them are two entirely distinct prospects."

"Undoubtedly. So?"

He compressed a sigh. "You are…"

"American, yes, I know. And tougher than steel boots."
She reached down and lifted her bag up, hoisting it over one
shoulder. "So? I'm ready when you are."

He walked towards her, his fingers clasping over the bag,
sliding it down her shoulder.

"You cannot come with me."

Her eyes locked to his, her chin tilted to angle her face
upwards. "You don't want me to come?"

His expression shifted, as the empty, lonely nights of his
last foray into the desert played out before him. "It is not a
trip of pleasure. The tribe is a long ride from here, in the hot
sun."

"I like the heat."

He ground his teeth together, his jaw moving with the
action. "That sun would peel this delicate, creamy skin from
your body in no time." He softened the words by dropping
his head and pressing a kiss to her lips. Just a gentle brush of
his mouth to hers but enough to set her alight. Never mind
the sun burning her skin – his touch was enough to incinerate her!

"I'm coming with you." It was a simple ultimatum. She
lifted her eyes to his and he shook his head.

"You are headstrong."

"So?"

He laughed, but it was a sound of impatience. "I don't
have time to do this with you now."

She felt the weight of worries on his shoulder and
frowned. "What's happened?"

He lifted his face away, focusing on the sun-filled day
beyond the window.

"It's complex."

"And what? I'm too simple to understand?" She snapped
with sarcasm.

He made a clicking sound of frustration. "I didn't say that.

Only right now, I need to get out there, not to be here with you…"

"Take me with you." She challenged him. "You can fill me in on the way."

She lifted her bag once more, side-stepping her man-mountain of a husband and moving towards the door. When she turned back, he was staring at her, a look on his face she couldn't interpret.

"You have no idea what you are asking for."

The words were said simply but with an undercurrent of sympathy that goaded Sophia into straightening her spine and locking her shoulders squarely into place.

"You married me. We didn't speak, before the wedding, about the kind of Sheikha I want to be. Well, this is it. I'm not ornamental, Malik. I don't want to sit in this lovely palace wearing beautiful dresses and tiaras, taking tea with the wives of foreign dignitaries." Her eyes sparked with his. "I've studied this country, its people, its politics. I come from a long line of American senators. I have instincts for this stuff. I'm coming with you."

He didn't speak for a long moment and she waited, with bated breath.

"These people live a completely different life to what you're used to."

"I know all about Bedouin traditions."

"Knowing about them and seeing them are two different things. You would not be able to speak to me like this in front of them."

She waited, a bag over her shoulder. "I wouldn't speak to you like this in front of anyone – and nor would you to me. No one needs to know the acrimonious state of our marriage behind closed doors."

She'd been making a statement of fact, but his eyes narrowed and something like anger crossed his features.

"Abu Faya is a modern country, here in the cities. But out there, the ancient laws and ways prevail. Women are not seen to have the value you presume to be your birthright."

"Of course it's my birthright. Don't stand there and act like you disagree with gender equality."

He dipped his head in silent concession.

"They are old fashioned. Every generation brings them closer in step but it cannot be forced. It is a fine balance. You are…"

"If you're worried that taking me out there will be like setting a cat amongst the pigeons, don't be. I understand the line you must be walk. I understand that my role, while in the desert, will be to appear somewhat… submissive."

He didn't speak but his eyes showed absolute disbelief.

"I get it. The culture of the tribes is different. I understand."

"Do you?" His eyes roamed her face and something shifted inside of her, because she would have put money on the fact he was angry about this, angry about the idea of her needing to appear even slightly subjugated, simply because of her gender.

"Addan hated that it would be necessary, but he explained everything to me."

"What did my brother explain?" He asked, the words thick and unnatural.

"That I would need to walk separate to my husband. That I would only be able to partake in morning coffee and evening *yashal* with you. That I would be left to speak to the women of the tribe." Her eyes glowed. "And still I want to go."

A muscle jerked at the base of his jaw.

"I am your wife," she said simply. "Don't deny me a chance to see all of this country, all of its people."

He crossed the room to her, wrapping his hands around

her upper arms and holding her still, so he could look into her eyes. "It's dangerous out there, completely unlike anything you've ever experienced."

She met his eyes, her lips compressed in a line of determination. "I am not afraid, Malik."

He stared down at her, a pulse of awareness throbbing between them, and then he shook his head. "Fine. But on one condition."

"Yes?"

"From this moment on, you do everything I say. Understood?"

She smiled, a smile that showed not even a hint of subservience. "Yes, your highness."

OF COURSE, plans had to be changed to allow for the fact his wife was accompanying him. Instead of riding out, he arranged for helicopters. It was far more sensible, in any event – the sooner he could get to the *Jakari* the sooner he could resolve this.

And he wanted the issue dealt with, once and for all.

The helicopter lifted up, over the desert, and beside him, Sophia craned forward, looking over the landscape with undisguised interest. Malik was less interested in the landscape and more interested in his wife.

As a child, she'd been chaotic and loud, running around the palace like a fairy, always laughing. As an adult woman, she was calmer, but captivating in equal measure – and for different reasons.

He closed his eyes for a moment and imagined living in another reality. He imagined Addan had lived, had he not been hell bent on restoring that piece of equipment and making it fly once more. He imagined that this woman was his brother's wife, and every fibre in his body rejected the idea of any other man possessing her.

His chest tightened to think that the cold war they'd been engaged in would have continued with that marriage, that Malik's self-imposed exile would have continued, all to avoid seeing her.

That this woman had been chosen to marry into his family had never made sense to him, but for the first time, seeing her determination to come with him to the Jakari people, something seemed to click in place.

She was fearless.

Fearless and brave, in the way of his people. She mightn't have come from these deserts, its ancient blood didn't hum in her body, but there was a spirit of strength about her that was familiar to Malik.

And Addan had seen that. He had seen it even when she'd been a little girl and he, Addan, a twelve year old. Or perhaps he'd simply trusted their father.

Malik had not. He'd fought this for as long as he could remember. He'd fought her inclusion into their family, her easy acceptance as part of the palace. He'd railed against her on every level.

And here they were – the only two left, side by side, the country's future in their hands.

"Look," she turned to face him, but her voice was barely audible above the sound of the rotor blades.

He lifted the pillow of the seat between them and pulled out two headsets, reaching across and hooking hers in place, barely resisting the impulse to run his thumb over her lower lip. He hooked his own headset in place then leaned over, so he could see what she was pointing at. It brought his body close to hers, and a surge of awareness began to beat inside of him.

Even now, even with the situation he was flying into, he

wanted her in a way that defied explanation. He ached for her, every single part of him was throbbing with that need.

"Is that the oasis of *Manama?*"

She turned to look at him, their faces separated by only an inch. "Yes."

He felt her eyes scanning his face, and straightened, but kept his gaze on the beautiful spot beneath the chopper. Crystal clear blue water formed a perfect oval, with palm trees lining one edge, and white sand on the other. There was a small rock formation a couple of hundred metres away, and a cave in one of them provided perfect natural shelter.

"Addan loved it there," she said, which quelled the desire in his stomach, if only a little.

"Yes." He sat back in his seat, staring straight ahead. "We used to go there often as children."

"He told me." She turned her face to his; he continued looking straight ahead. "He told me you ran away there when you were fifteen, determined to live out your days in that cave."

A smile twitched at the corners of Malik's mouth. "I wasn't quite so recalcitrant as that makes me sound."

"No? Were you sulking over something, Malik?" She teased, and now he shifted his gaze to her, his eyes landing on her lips. Parted and pink, he found them impossibly distracting.

"I don't remember now," he lied.

"But you've always liked the desert," she said softly. "Addan said you were at one with it. As though you have been cast from it by magic."

Malik shook his head. "My brother was poetic with his words."

"I think he was speaking the truth," she demurred. "You would have been at home living out here, wouldn't you?"

A muscle jerked in his jaw. "Contemplating hypotheticals is a futile waste of energy."

"I don't know," she murmured, biting down on her lip. "I think it's instructive."

"As to what?"

"Who you are."

His lips formed a gash in his face. "I find the freedom of the desert compelling. So too the elemental nature of it. Out here, it is man and earth, and one has to be prepared to survive on merit."

He saw the smile whisper across her face. "You're so different to Addan."

His gut tightened. He looked away from her, out over the desert. What would have taken him a day on horseback was under an hour in flight time. With a wife determined to psychoanalyse him and compare him to Addan? It felt considerably longer.

"Yes." The agreement was crisp. He hoped it would put an end to the conversation.

It didn't, of course. He had already learned that when Sophia set her mind on something, she let very little stand in her way. "You were close growing up but not as teenagers," she said.

That had him turning to face her. "I considered Addan to be my best friend."

"No, he was my best friend," she said softly. "He hardly saw you."

A muscle throbbed in Malik's jaw and regrets fizzed in his blood.

"You were always out here. Or overseas. Sewing your wild oats, he would say."

Malik's eyes slammed shut. Is that what his brother had thought? That Malik had chosen to travel and sleep around with beautiful women rather than being home, shouldering his responsibilities? "Unlike Addan, I was not tied to Abu Faya. The freedom to travel was always my right."

"Of course," she nodded. "He missed you, though."

Malik's stomach clenched. Fury slashed his insides. There was no going back, no changing the decisions he'd made and the way he'd handled his life.

"He loved you."

"Stop." His eyes swept shut for a moment. "Do not speak to me of Addan. At least, do not speak to me of his feelings for me. I know what we were to each other. I know how he felt."

"He was proud of you," she said simply.

"Stop," he repeated, this time holding a hand in the air to silence her. "Respect me, respect my wishes, Sheikha."

"Or what? You'll have me flown back to the palace? Why won't you talk to me about him? Does it occur to you that you're the only other person who loved him as I did? Who I can share my grief with?"

Malik felt as though his chest had been cleaved wide open. "Get a therapist, Sophia, if you want to talk out your grief."

"Jeez," she whispered, spinning her face away from his, looking out the window. But not fast enough – he saw the tears that sparkled on her lashes and knew he'd done that to her. Guilt chewed at his heels.

"He loved you," she whispered. "He hated that you and I… that we weren't… he hated that we hated each other. He wanted us to be friends. But how can we be? How can we be anything other than this when you are determined to be so…"

He waited, his pulse like a volcano. "Yes?"

"So cold." She finished, shaking her head. "Everywhere except bed."

The words settled on his shoulders, and they felt right.

They felt good, somehow, the limitations exactly what his relationship with his brother's fiancé *should* have been.

"You chose this marriage," he reminded her, surprising even himself with how arctic the words sounded. "Knowing what it would be like."

"I thought he'd been right about you. I thought if I got to know you better…"

"He was wrong. You were wrong. This is who I am, this is what I want from our marriage. I'm sorry to be pain you, naturally, but do not look to change me, Sheikha."

She bit down on her lip and he suspected it was to stop a sob from emerging. "I won't." She stared straight ahead for the remainder of the flight.

CHAPTER 9

I T WAS HOTTER AND more unpleasant than anything she'd ever experienced, like being a turkey in the oven on Thanksgiving Day, no reprieve in sight. Even the breeze that occasionally rolled lackadaisically past was warm, offering no respite from the searing heat.

But she didn't express, with words nor gesture, that she was even remotely uncomfortable.

The helicopter had set down hours earlier, followed by a second, which set up an enormous tent for her and Malik, a little away from the ramshackle group of Bedouin constructions. Theirs was sturdy and designed for comfort – even a small bathroom had been constructed – a rudimentary shower head and toilet meant the creature comforts she'd neglected to consider were of no concern.

There were more clothes for her too, and she was immensely glad, because none of what she'd brought was suitable. The singlet tops she'd planned to wear revealed far too much skin, for modesty but also sunburn. Instead, she changed into one of the long, flowing robes with sleeves that fell to her wrists, and which were made of a very fine linen weave, meaning what little breeze there was could pass through her.

She scooped her hair out of the pony-tail and opted for a bun instead, trying to maximize the places the stilted desert air could reach her.

Malik had disappeared the moment they'd touched down. He'd strode out of the helicopter without so much as a backwards glance and she'd fought an urge to pitch herself after him, to run at him and throw her fists against his chest and to shout at him to stop being such a dictatorial bastard and open up to her! Addan was their common ground. His death had affected them both. Why wouldn't he talk to her about that?

She sipped the ice cold tea that had been prepared for her – several servants had been brought to the desert as well, though they were staying in the Bedouin tribe.

Sophia knew this wasn't how Malik travelled, when he ventured into the desert. She'd learned from Addan that he slept under the stars as much as possible, occasionally setting up a simple tent for himself – usually only when one of the desert's fiery sandstorms were expected, to save his skin from being sheared off.

So all of this, then, was for her.

And that infuriated her. She didn't want special treatment. Okay, maybe she did. Maybe the toilet and the shower were a nice touch. But she didn't want him to think she was some precious little wildflower that needed protecting. She was his wife – his equal – and he had to start treating her like that.

Or maybe she was just furious with him in general, frustrated by his insistence on keeping her at arm's length even when they'd shared something so special, so meaningful. Because it was meaningful, wasn't it? Sex was sex, sure. She got it.

But it hadn't been 'just sex'. Not even when he'd insisted as much. There was no way the passion that had burst between them was normal or routine. It had to be because of who they were. She had no experience, no point of comparison, and yet she felt it with complete certainty. So why wasn't he admitting that?

She let out a grating noise of frustration at the moment a noise sounded from the flap of her tent.

"Excuse me?" The voice came to her in Abu Fayan, but the accent was thick.

She stood up, moving towards the flap of the tent, fanning her face as she walked.

"Hello?"

The woman on the other side was around her age, with dark hair, dark eyes, and a kind smile. "Hi."

She bowed low, then straightened. "Am I intruding?"

"Not at all. Would you like to come in?"

"I cannot." Her expression was wry. "This is only for you and your husband." She took a step backwards. "I wondered if you might like to come and see the ruins of *Persimina*. They are only an hour or so from here, and I have provisions."

Sophia was intrigued. "I've never heard of them. I'm sorry, who are you?"

The other woman laughed. "Forgive me, I presumed my reputation had preceded me. I am Saliyah. Also known as the reason you're here."

"His highness hasn't really told me why we're here," she said apologetically, patching together what she did know of these people, and their desperate bid to stop their young from fleeing the settlement and moving to the cities. She could only presume this woman wished to do likewise.

"Then I can tell you on the way." She pulled the flap wider. "As for the ruins, they are a thousand years old – one of the earliest buildings, and quite dramatic. You will enjoy seeing them."

"What on earth was built all the way out here?"

"The beginnings of a castle, at one time," Saliyah murmured, stepping back to allow Sophia to follow her. She whistled and a camel sauntered over. "Have you ever been on a camel?"

A memory came flashing back to her and she laughed, spontaneously. Addan had given her one for her nineteenth birthday, as a joke. She'd fallen right off it. "Yes, and not very successfully."

"We have horses if you'd prefer? Only there is a small watering hole near the ruins and the camels are thirsty…"

"It's fine. I'll be fine." She eyed the beast thoughtfully. "Only… how do I…?"

"Grab here," Saliyah nodded towards a braided cord that was dangling around the camel's neck. "And swing up."

It took Sophia two attempts but then she was sat between the humps, feeling apprehensive, but proud. Belatedly, she thought of Malik. "Will we be long? If later than dusk I should inform my husband…"

"We will be back before the *yashal*."

Sophia nodded. "Which way?"

Saliyah's smile was enigmatic. "He knows."

The camel began to step forward and Sophia gripped the braided chord that ran around his head a little tighter, fear lurching through her.

This was different to the camel Addan had surprised her with. Calmer. Perhaps more used to conveying passengers, or maybe worn down by the heat of the desert. He took a sedate path, walking easily, and Saliyah's camel kept pace beside.

"You are younger than I expected," Saliyah observed, as some distance emerged between them and the settlement.

"Am I? What did you expect?"

The sun beat down; Sophia resisted the temptation to wipe sweat from her brow.

"I don't know." Saliyah laughed. "I should say, you are young to have a position of such responsibility."

Sophia didn't point out that at the moment her role was largely ceremonial – and one of breeding. Her smile was tight.

"How old are you, Saliyah?"

"Twenty one."

Sophia shifted her gaze sideways, easily able to look at her companion. The camel continued on its course. "And you want to leave the tribe?"

Saliyah's eyes flicked to Sophia's and then she looked straight ahead, her expression one of stone. "Yes."

"But Laith does not wish this?" Sophia pushed, trying to understand what her husband wouldn't speak to her about.

Saliyah's laugh lacked humour. "He has threatened to imprison my parents if I leave."

Sophia drew in a harsh breath. "Why?"

"Because our numbers can't keep dropping. Because if my entire generation chooses to leave the tribe, or worse, run away, there will be no one left to bring new children into this way of life. He is only trying to protect our people from the incursion of that." She jabbed a thumb towards the desert, beyond which were the cities and the future. "The twenty first century is suffocating us all."

The image Saliyah painted was poignant. "The twenty first century is a reality to be grappled with," Sophia said slowly, thoughtfully. "Speaking as a person, not as Sheikha, I cannot see Laith – or anyone – can stand in the doorway of change and hope to stop it."

Saliya's dark eyes sparked with Sophia's. "Nor can I." She sighed. "I do not want the tribe to fall apart. I do not want my generation's legacy to be this – our elderly alone out here, to fend for themselves and to live out the ancient ways of our people with no hope of those rites continuing. But I want to study. I have always wanted to learn and understand. I was fortunate. My father procured books for me, lots of books, from a trader who we cross paths with three times a year. On each occasion, father would swap what books we had, and more would be brought."

Sophia's smile was warm. "I also love to read."

"There is no greater pleasure," Saliyah sighed.

Sophia nodded, thinking of how many times in her life she'd escaped into books, fallen into their pages to avoid the reality that surrounded her.

"As I grew older, he began to bring school books. Texts. Long papers and dissertations. I think he saw that my mind was enquiring and wanted to foster that in some way. A year ago, he brought an exam from a university. He and my father argued, but the trader was adamant. My mother too. They persuaded my father to let me at least sit the paper, to complete what I could of it."

"And?"

Sophia was so hot, her cheeks bright pink. Saliyah reached into the bag that hung on the camel's side and pulled out a flat-shaped bottle. "Here." She passed it over; Sophia took it gratefully.

Cool water was within. She drank and replaced the lid, handing it back to Saliyah.

"How did you do on the test?"

"The university said it was a perfect score. They couldn't believe I've never had any formal education. They offered me a place, a full scholarship, with board." She turned to Sophia, her expression overflowing with emotion. "I'm terrified to go, your highness. I have no idea what a city is like – the trader told me it is noisier than when all of the night birds cry together, and never ending – but I know I have to do this."

Sophia nodded slowly. "And Laith is determined that you will not go?"

"Yes." Saliyah's voice showed sadness. "And I cannot leave here knowing that my parents will suffer."

"Of course you can't." She ran the palm of her hand over the camel's neck, lost in thought. "My husband is progressive. I'm confident he'll make Laith see sense."

"What if he doesn't?"

"He will," Sophia promised, her eyes showing determination. "I'll make sure of that."

"What do you mean, you do not know where she is?" Malik glared at the servants who'd been assigned to his wife, his expression one of fire and ice.

"She was resting!" The first proclaimed, not meeting Malik's furious gaze. "And did not want to be disturbed."

A muscle jerked in Malik's jaw as he tried to constrain his temper. All afternoon, he'd butted heads with Laith and now, to return to his tent and find his wife lost? "We are in the desert," he said with cold derision. "She has no knowledge of this place, of our ways, of this climate. There are eagles circling the outer reaches. Desert dogs that will tear a person from limb to limb. And you let her wander off?"

The Sheikh had never lost his temper before. His servants were struck dumb.

"Find her," he roared. And then, "Power up the helicopter. I'll find her myself."

He strode from the tent just as a little girl from the community came running up, speaking rapidly and in a childish way that made comprehension difficult. "Look!" She pointed, her finger jerking. In the distance, Malik could see two camels loping slowly towards them.

Dusk was approaching, the light was dim, but he could still make out his wife's pale blonde hair as clearly as if she were standing before him. Damn her!

"Bring me a horse," he snapped, not moving his gaze from her. He could only stare at her, a sense of powerful fury and rage surging through him. Where the hell had she been? And with whom?

"That is Saliyah," Laith grumbled, appearing at Malik's side, holding the reins to an Arabian stud.

Malik didn't offer a response. He threw his body onto the horse's back, kicked its sides and tore through the desert, plumes of sand in his wake.

The camels moved slowly but the horse was all speed. He closed the gap on them in minutes, bringing his horse to them, his eyes fixed on his wife's. She'd obviously seen his approach and had time to prepare, for there was only defiance in her expression, willing him to challenge her.

Oh, and he would. But not now.

"Saliyah," he addressed the tribe girl. "You had no business abducting my wife."

"She hardly abducted me, Malik—,"

He slid his gaze to his wife. "You, I will speak to privately." The words were loaded with ice. He returned his attention to the young woman whose future he'd been discussing all day. "You are in enough trouble without adding kidnap to the charge sheet."

"Oh, because she wants to do what any ordinary teenager wishes to do?" Sophia interjected, apparently not willing to be silenced.

Malik compressed his lips.

"Go ahead of us to camp. Laith is waiting."

Saliyah's expression was ash.

"She is not to be in trouble for this," Sophia said firmly. "She asked if I wanted to see the ruins of Persimina. I did. It was very kind of Saliyah to entertain me."

"The ruins?" Malik looked from one to the other. "That's what you've been doing?"

Sophia tilted her chin.

"You still should have told someone," he pushed, his expression unrelenting. "Her highness cannot simply climb onto a camel and set out into the desert. Did you think about the risks to her, Saliyah? She has no experience of this climate, the animals here, the heat…"

"*She*," Sophia interjected, "was fine. And Saliyah brought water and food and hats and some kind of whistle that I gather is supposed to sound an alarm in case of danger."

It was all so reasonable, but Malik was still furious.

"Go back to camp. Tell Laith my wife chose to come with you freely," he said to Saliyah, moving closer to Sophia's camel and reaching for her reins. "I will join you for the *yashal*."

Once Saliyah was far enough ahead, Malik moved their animals, yet chose a different path to that which Saliyah had taken. He circumnavigated the constellation of Bedouin tents, bringing them around behind the settlement, directly to their private accommodations.

He didn't speak.

He didn't trust himself to, until they were alone.

At the door to their tent, there were guards.

"Move out," he snapped, as they approached. The guards saluted and stepped back to a wider proximity. He didn't look at his wife but he knew she was right behind him. He held the tent flap wide for her, his gaze fixed into the distance. Only once she was inside did he turn his gaze on her, flicking it from the tip of her head over her sun-warmed cheeks and down her body.

And every feeling known to man burst through him. Desire, foremost. Anger. Fury. Impatience. Desperation.

He stepped into the tent, sucking in a deep breath, tying a knot in the braids that kept the flaps shut. And then he rounded on her, his expression a mask of fury.

"Do not ever do something like that again."

She was completely unrepentant. If anything, he felt an equal anger emanating from her.

"Like what?" She demanded, reaching for the long-sleeved shirt she wore and stripping it from her body.

"What are you doing?"

"I'm hot! Stinking hot, okay?" She flung the shirt across the tent; it landed on the edge of the bed that had been laid out for her.

"You cannot simply disappear whenever you feel like it."

"I went to explore some ruins with someone from the tribe. You trust these people? You like them? Why shouldn't I?"

"She could have kidnapped you and held you to ransom for her own freedom!"

"She should never be in a position of needing to do that," Sophia roared, her vehemence surprising him. "If a woman is driven to such desperate measures courtesy of an oppression you are facilitating, then she is hardly the problem, even if she *were* to have taken such desperate measures."

He was, momentarily, shocked into silence. But her nakedness reminded him of the purpose of this marriage, the reason for their union.

"Do you forget, *Sharafaha*, that you may well carry this country's future heir in your belly?"

He saw surprise whip across her features. "So?" But it was less vehement.

"So your life is no longer your own to do with as you please. You married me. You are this country's Sheikha.

People are looking to you for our future. You cannot simply ride off into a desert about which you know nothing –,"

"I was not alone!" She interrupted forcefully.

But that only angered him further. "You had no concept of what dangers were out there. Beasts, birds, Saliyah…"

"She was no threat to me!" Sophia snapped, lifting her fingers to her temples and rubbing them gently. She turned away, moving to the pitcher of water and pouring some into her hands, hands that were shaking slightly. She lifted the water to her face, splashing her sun-reddened cheeks.

"And how did you ascertain this, Sophia?" He asked, moving closer, his large body held taut, his gut throbbing with needs and wants that made no sense given his anger.

"I…"

"Did you speak to security about her? Did you ask for details about her? Did you do *anything* to ensure you weren't riding off into the desert with a madwoman? Potentially with our baby growing in your belly?"

Her gaze dropped to the ground.

He moved closer, an arm clamping around her waist, drawing her body to his.

She gasped, her eyes lifting to his, and now he felt that she was trembling all over, like she had been right before their wedding.

"Did you think about what you owe me, and this country? What you owe Addan?"

At that, she made a strangled noise of disbelief, her eyes lifting to his.

"Damn you, Sophia. Did you think how *I* would feel? Coming back here and finding you missing?"

She opened her mouth, perhaps to explain, perhaps to argue. He didn't wait to find out. He dropped his mouth to hers, claiming her lips, his kiss hard and demanding. It was a kiss of punishment. A kiss of anger.

It was also a kiss of survival.

"Damn it," he groaned, lifting her, wrapping her legs around his waist, his body hard for her, his mind still running over the fear he'd felt when he'd discovered she was missing.

"You cannot simply disappear on a whim." He dropped her onto the low mattress and crouched at her feet, but even as he reached for her underwear, she was wriggling out of it, her hands fevered, her breath escaping in fast, desperate bursts.

"It wasn't a whim!" Her hands glided over his back, finding his hips, holding him tight. "I was just…"

"Don't." The word was like a whip; he pushed up, his face level with hers, his eyes showing impatience. "Don't say anything. There is no excuse for this, *Sharafaha*. You were wrong to leave here with her. Wrong to leave without alerting me. Wrong not to take a security guard. You are a Queen, Sophia, not some American tourist on a gap year. Start acting like it."

She lifted up onto her elbows, glaring at him as he pushed out of his clothes. Her eyes dropped to his chest, her mouth dry – as though it were filled with sawdust. "That is incredibly unreasonable. I *am* a Queen. Just because I don't conform to any ridiculous standards you have of what that should entail… well, newsflash, your highness. Being accessible to your people isn't a bad thing. And I know you agree with me because look at how you live! You come out here *all* the time. You love to just be by yourself with these tribes. So why can't I?"

"Because you could right this moment be pregnant with my child, Sophia. Do you not think that requires some consideration?"

She clamped her lips shut, because his observation was accurate – and she hadn't stopped to consider that...

"And because you are not me," he finished, growling the words with a low, deep husk.

"So I don't have the same privileges as you?"

"No." The word was said with sheer frustration. He brought his body over hers, his eyes locked in a battle of the wills with her pale blue gaze. "You begged me to bring you here. Fool that I am I thought you would respect the desert and its inherent dangers. I thought you would at least respect the difficult political situation we are in."

"How is talking to Saliyah disrespecting that?" She demanded, her breath ragged, so her pert breasts moved up and down of their own accord. He brought a hand between her legs, spreading them wide.

"Because I am trying to get Laith to make this decision for himself," Malik muttered.

"And if he makes the wrong decision?"

He rolled his tongue over one of her nipples and arrows of pleasure perforated her veins, filling her body with shark sparks of desire.

"Precisely why I am handling this with delicacy."

But temptation and need had overtaken common sense. Sophia wanted to argue for Saliyah but rational thought was so far from possible.

Acting purely on instinct, she arched her back, the tip of his arousal so close to her womanhood. She wanted to beg him to take her, but the words stayed buried in her throat.

But he understood anyway. He stared into her eyes as he thrust deep inside her, hard and fast, so she dug her nails into his shoulder and bit back from crying out his name – damn her – knowing how much he needed to hear it.

He dropped his mouth forward and took her lower lip between his teeth, biting down on it to tease her.

She almost swore in surprise and he laughed, kissing her

more gently. But it was Sophia who fired back, mashing her lips to his with all-consuming need.

He thrust into her again, the motion firm. Her body writhed beneath his, and suddenly, he could think only of this. Only of her.

He swore in his mind as he dropped his head to her breast, running his teeth over her nipples, his finger and thumb tormenting first one and then turning to the other, until she was moaning over and over. He thrust into her, his body dominating hers, and yet it wasn't enough.

He needed... He needed to make her crazier than she'd ever been. He needed her to understand how terrified he'd been to come into this tent and find her missing. Those moments of her absence, before she'd been sighted, had filled him with ice. He needed to make love to her now to over-write those fears.

"You should not have left the camp."

She closed her eyes, her body quivering, a mess of desire.

He thrust into her, his possession absolute and she made a low, moaning sound of surrender, of acceptance.

He pulled out, bringing his hand between her legs, teasing her most sensitive cluster of nerves. "You are to be kept safe. Even if that means locking you in the tower in which we spent our wedding night and throwing away the key."

"Are you actually threatening to imprison me?" She demanded breathily, her orgasm so close he could feel her nerves tingling.

He moved his hand away, bracing himself directly over her.

"Yes," he said, simply. "If that's what it takes." And he drove himself into her, and her tight, wet core spasmed around his length as she exploded. He felt her come and he kissed her, tasting her exhalations, her cries, and swallowing them deep inside of himself.

"I am no one's prisoner," she moaned, as he lifted up from her.

He begged to differ. He thrust into her and she made a small keening noise of pleasure.

"Come here." He stood, pulling away from her reluctantly, and moving to the small dressing table that had been set up along the edge of the tent. An ornate mirror hung at its centre.

He watched her in it, watched as she walked to him, her slender body marked with the signs of their lovemaking, which made his whole body jerk with renewed pleasures.

"Do you remember our wedding night?" He asked, positioning her in front of him.

She swallowed, her delicate throat moving visibly.

He held her hips, bending her forward so her arms were supported on the dressing table, then used her hair to pull her head up a little, so her eyes were level with the mirror.

"Watch what I can do to you, and tell me you're not a prisoner to this." He spread her hips wide, and thrust into her from behind. Heat contorted her features, stretching her lips, widening her eyes, colouring her cheeks. "Watch what you can do to me," he groaned, as he buried himself deeper inside of her than ever before, his face tight, his expression almost pained. "And tell me I am not also a prisoner to this madness?"

CHAPTER 10

"THE *YASHAL* IS SOMETHING no outsiders ever get to see," he murmured from where he sat beside her, their position separate to the tribe, set apart, honoured guests. They were on a bright burgundy carpet, with flickering gold candles spread about them. Sweet wine had been brought, and dried fruits which tasted like honey and vanilla.

Sophia watched as the tribe danced, ancient instruments being plucked to create a magical music, and darkness began to fall over the deserts, the stars shining in the heavens above.

She watched the way the tribe men and women danced, their bodies seeming to capture the desert winds, the ancient sands, the music itself. It was breathtakingly beautiful, but her mind was only half there.

Every time she blinked, she saw them.

Malik and her, the way he'd taken her from behind, his powerful body driving anything from her head and heart, making her exist purely for that moment. And she saw the truth in his words – that they were both of them a prisoner to this desire.

She sat beside her husband, and remembered everything. The way he'd always made her feel. The way his eyes had seemed to sear her from the inside out. As a teenager, she'd mistaken it for animosity. But now that she'd felt their incendiary connection, she had to admit – to herself at least – that it was so much more.

She'd wanted him for a long time. She'd desired him. She'd seen him with other women and hated him, hated them. On some kind of primal level, her body had craved his for years.

She turned to face him. He was staring straight ahead, his profile enigmatic. And then he shifted his gaze, suddenly, jerking it towards her, and her breath snagged in her throat.

They'd hated each other.

Except, what if they hadn't?

Was it possible he'd desired her too? That he'd felt the same rush of need? Only she'd been younger and inexperienced, and had misunderstood what that feeling meant. But Malik? He was hardly a virgin. Surely he'd recognized it for desire?

It wasn't possible that the strength of this, of what they felt, had sprung up out of nowhere. The simmering tension between them, the ever-present cold war, surely that had more to do with repressed need than anything else?

"If you keep looking at me like that, I will find a tent to drag you in to…" he warned, his lips twisting slightly in the corners, showing him to be joking.

Her smile was enigmatic. "Do you think I'd complain?"

And his smile dropped as the full force of desire sledged him from the sides and she knew, with absolute certainty, that the real fight they'd been waging all these years wasn't about him not liking her and her not liking him. It was about this.

About them wanting each other and having no way to express it.

They'd both been a prisoner to this desire for years.

It all made sense.

And Addan?

Guilt sliced through her stomach. If he'd lived, she'd be married to him now. Happily married.

Except...

She whipped her head away, focusing on the dancers, her eyes filling unexpectedly with tears. Would she have really been happy?

She'd have been *content*. Was that the same as happiness? Was this?

She reached for her wine, taking a small sip and replacing the goblet, her eyes lifting to Malik's of their own volition. He was watching her, a heated possession in his gaze that curled her toes.

"I've always thought you hated me," she said quietly, moving a little closer so their conversation wouldn't carry on the desert winds to any of the tribes people.

He kept his focus on the dancers.

"But you had no reason to hate me, did you?"

"You were marrying my brother," he said cryptically. "And I could never understand why."

"So you acted like you hated me?"

A muscle jerked in his jaw. She lifted a fingertip to it without thinking, and his head turned slowly to hers. "I have acted as I felt," he said simply, confusing her, because maybe she was wrong. Maybe the desire was all on her. Maybe she'd craved him for many, many years, and he'd simply resented her.

"You are a beautiful, intelligent American woman with the world at her feet. You have considerable personal fortune at your disposal, so I know you did not agree to this marriage for wealth. Why? What would make a young person decide to turn her back on her own culture and exist in the servitude of another?"

"You think this is servitude?" She asked quietly.

"It is not freedom."

Her heart twisted. "You hate this, don't you? Being Sheikh."

"It is an honour," he clipped.

"But one you could do without."

He shook his head. "There is no sense discussing hypotheticals. The crown is Addan's. I am simply minding it for our child. A caretaker."

"Don't do that," she said, leaning forward of her body's own volition. "Don't diminish what you bring to this. Addan always said you were a natural leader. That you should have been the first born."

Malik compressed his lips, and looked away. "Addan didn't wish to rule."

"No," Sophia's smile was wistful. "I know."

Malik was quiet for a long moment. "He wanted to study. Philosophy."

"He was a terrible philosopher though," Sophia giggled. "He could never tell his Plato from his Ptolemy…"

Malik was still. "I'll take your word for it."

"Kindness and goodness were his philosophies," she said, softening, sobering. "But Malik? He was right. Between the two of you, yours is the temperament more given to ruling. And I think you know that. I think you've always known it. Is that why you stayed away so much? So as not to crowd him?"

Malik's jaw tightened. "I believe we've discussed how I feel about you psychoanalyzing me."

"I'm just trying to make sense of everything," she promised.

"There is no sense that can be made of his death." He

turned to face her, and now there was a strength and deter-mination in his expression. "Why did you agree to this marriage? Why did your mother consent?"

"My mother?" Sophia pulled a face. "My mother had very little interest in what Arabella or I did. She was just glad we were off her hands."

"But your father actively willed this. He negotiated with my father for this event."

"Yes," Sophia nodded thoughtfully.

"But you were only young when he died. There was no compulsion on you to go through with it."

"He wanted it," she said quietly. "Your father told me again and again how they had discussed this union, imag-ining me on the throne."

"I see," Malik nodded, his brain almost visibly cogitating this development.

"I don't think I really made a conscious decision. It just felt... right."

"And you felt closer to your father by accepting," he murmured.

"I..." it was perceptive. She dipped her head forward, hiding her eyes, but his finger and thumb caught her chin, lifting her face to his.

"Don't hide from me."

Her eyes sparked to his. "I'm not." She sighed. "It's just... not as simple as that."

"So explain to me."

It was a command, and at any other time, she might have smiled, for how it completely reinforced what she'd just been thinking, about how well he took charge, how naturally he lead.

"I... my father died." The words were thick with grief, despite the fact it had been many years earlier. "We'd had the most perfect family, and then he got sick and everything was broken. Our mom went… kind of… I don't know. She was different. So we didn't just lose dad, we lost mom, too. And I had this memory of this perfect family, this sense of belonging that just evaporated overnight. Arabella went overseas, and I was so lonely." She bit down on her lower lip, watching the dancing without really seeing.

"And then I met Addan. And I was so broken, Malik. I was so sad and lost and he was so kind and I just felt like… like I'd come home." She shook her head sadly from side to side then brushed her cheek over her knee, turning to look at her husband. "I suppose that sounds ridiculous."

But there was an expression on his face that was impossible to interpret.

"I never really agreed to the marriage, so much as I felt more at home here than anywhere else. I felt that I belonged. Your dad, your brother, they loved me in a way I desperately needed – they were my family. Given the choice of staying here or going back to the states, it was an easy decision."

It was dark, but she could make out the harsh angles and planes on Malik's face. She felt the emotions swirling through him.

"I don't want to always be fighting with you," she said, simply. "I don't want our children to grow up in a war zone." She lifted a hand to his cheek, rubbing it over his skin tentatively. She felt him stiffen and frustration gnawed at her gut. Was she only allowed to touch him in the bedroom? Her voice grew hoarse. "Your father loved me. Your brother loved me. I'm going to be the mother to your child. Can you not at least try to accept me as part of your life?"

"I married you, didn't I?"

"Yes, and in bed, you treat me like your wife. But I want to be your equal here, too. I want this marriage to be real. I want us to be a family, Malik." She swallowed, having not realised until she spoke those words the importance of what she was feeling. "I don't want this to be a sham marriage."

He turned to face her and his eyes were loaded with darkness and pain.

"I cannot give you what you want, *Sharafaha.* And I won't make promises I have no intention of keeping."

"Why can't you at least try?" She dropped her hand from his face, turning back to the dancers, but all of her was homed in on the man beside her, every cell in her body attuned to his every movement.

"I inherited this marriage. For the sake of my kingdom and my people, we have wed. But I refuse to pretend this is anything more than it is: two people who require a child. Who have sex. Stop trying to dress our relationship up as something else. And for God's sake, stop comparing me to Addan. You will never find what you are looking for in me."

———

She had longed to see the desert, to explore all of the special places Addan had spoken to her of *ad infinitum*, but when morning broke, she was endlessly glad. So glad it was a new day, a day free of her foolish hopes for finding common ground with her husband. Free of any desire to make their marriage deeper, more meaningful.

All Sophia wanted, when she woke, was to get dressed and go back to the palace. Back to her own room, with all her books and her things, where she felt closest to herself. And most of all, she wanted not to see her husband.

No. That was a lie.

Even now, with her heart feeling bruised and weatherbeaten, she lay on the low mattress, conscious of his every breath, feeling his body shift beside hers, and she ached for him on a cellular level.

I refuse to pretend this is more than two people who require a child. Who have sex.

What had she expected?

That they'd marry and something magical would happen? That all the animosity between them would dissipate? That they'd sleep together and suddenly he'd unlock all her secrets, and she'd unlock his, and their future would be rosy and safe?

Her heart felt heavier and tears clogged her eyes once more.

It should have been Addan.

True, she'd never have known the mind-altering power of truly amazing sex, nor this lurching sensation in the region of her heart. But she would at least have known contentment.

She pushed the covers off and moved out of bed, but his arm caught her, snaking out so his fingers could wrap around her wrist, surprising her completely.

She startled, looking over her shoulder, wishing she hadn't when her heart began to pound at a billion miles an hour.

He saw everything, and she hated him that. His eyes raked her face, her body, clinging to the swell of her cleavage and then lifting to eyes that were still moist with tears.

"You're upset."

She shook her head. "I'm fine." She pulled away from him, standing, looking around the ornate tent. "When can we leave?"

"You were so impatient to come to the desert. You want to leave again after only one night?"

"Well, let's see," she put her hand on her hip and pretended to enumerate. "Since we've arrived you've left me on my own for hours, then berated me for going to explore some fascinating ruins, then told me I was being fanciful for even hoping we could have a relationship that extended beyond this," she gestured towards the bed, the tangle of sheets proof of the way he'd ravaged her the night before. "So forgive me if I'm not finding the desert as richly enjoyable as I'd hoped."

He pushed up to sitting, watching her through shuttered eyes.

"You knew I was coming here for business – I had no intention of bringing you, Sophia, so you'll forgive me for not being on hand to entertain you around the clock. As for your unscheduled touristing, yes, I berated you, and rightly so. My issue was not that you went but that you didn't have the insight to communicate your plans to a living soul. You are a person of extreme importance to this kingdom, never mind the fact you may well already be pregnant with my child."

He breathed in and his nostrils flared; she had the sense he was trying to rein in his own temper. "I was angry with your cavalier disregard for your safety. This is important. Being here is important. I cannot do what I must do if I'm worrying about you the whole time."

She ground her teeth together. "You don't have to worry about me. I was fine."

"That was better luck than management."

"You're so Goddamned arrogant," she snapped, shaking her head. "You honestly think I don't know how to look after myself?"

He clamped his lips together – she felt as though he were holding something back, something hurtful. She supposed she should be grateful he was at least trying to spare her feelings.

"I think you are a fish out of water here," he said after a lengthy pause. "I think my brother filled your head with myths and legends and neglected to tell you the truth about these lands. I think you have lived a charmed life and see everything through the veil of your innocence and exuberance, and that you can't perceive of a world where people do bad things, where some people are simply wholly bad."

"I beg your pardon!" She spat, cutting him off. "You know my life has been anything but charmed."

"You grew up in immense wealth, the adored daughter of a senator…"

"Who died when I was nine years old!" She shouted, then dragged a hand through her hair, desperately trying to cool her temper. "I lost everything when he died, Malik. I know plenty about sadness and…"

"Yes, but you do not know about civil wars and terrorist factions, both of which have existed here in Abu Faya, and within my lifetime. This country, while beautiful, is not always safe. And not for someone like you."

She let his words sink in, her features shifting to reflect her surprise. "I know that." She bit down on her lip. "I told you, I know all about this country's past."

"Then act like it," he said firmly. "If we have a child together, you will be responsible for ensuring that child's wellbeing. I cannot imagine you would send our heir riding off with a stranger…"

"Of course I wouldn't!"

"Then why take that risk for yourself?" He pressed a hand to her stomach. "Even if you are not pregnant, and you may not be, you are still my wife. You are the woman this country has adopted as its Sheikha. You must protect yourself for them."

She tilted her chin defiantly even when she felt a strong instinct to cry. "I trusted my instincts, Malik, and they were right. I liked Saliyah; I trusted her."

"But you could just as easily have been wrong." He ground his teeth together. "Addan loved you, *Sharafaha*." He stepped back from her a little, his shoulders broad, his back ramrod straight. "He would expect me to be protecting you from any dangers. Can't you see that? If you will not exercise caution at my behest, do so for Addan. Do it because he would have expected it of you."

She turned away from him, moving towards the table that had a pitcher of water set up on it. She poured herself a glass and held it between trembling fingertips. "Addan trusted I could look after myself." She turned to face him, and her expression was tense, her skin pale. "He would *never* have shouted at me like you did."

A muscle throbbed low in Malik's jaw. "No, he wouldn't. Addan was perfect, and I am not – we have established that fact many times. I am simply trying to do what's best for you, Sophia."

"Don't you think I have a say in that?"

He held her gaze for a long time and then shook his head, simply. "I am the King of this land, and you are my wife. I'm afraid when it comes to your security and protection, you will just have to get used to doing as I say."

"So I'm, what? Yours to command?"

His eyes glinted in his face, his handsome, distracting face. "You probably do not wish to know how appealing I find that description right now."

And just like that, the anger in her belly swirled and vibrated, morphing into something else, something far more tense and distracting, something that robbed her of breath.

His laugh was soft. "See, Sophia? Do not be so concerned by the fact we are not 'friends'. You want me, even when you hate me. True?"

She glared at him, but her pulse was racing and there was an inferno raging between her legs. Pointedly, his eyes dropped to her breasts, and she felt the sting of her nipples as they hardened against the flimsy linen of her nightgown.

"If I touched you right now, you'd fall apart in my arms. Why do you fight this?"

Anger stoked through the desire. "Because you're an arrogant piece of work and someone ought to put you in your place."

He laughed at that, closing the distance between them, his powerful body dwarfing hers. "Tell me you don't want me," he said, simply, reaching for her nightgown and lifting it over her head.

She continued to glare at him, her lower lip very close to a pout.

"Say it. Tell me you don't want me and I will walk out of this tent right now, and leave you to get ready for the day."

She opened her mouth to say something, but the words died inside of her. Sophia had always been a fighter, but she couldn't fight this. She didn't *want* to fight this. In a world that had left her bereft, that had stripped her of almost everyone she loved, had made her alone and lonely, she had this. She had Malik. And he wasn't everything she wanted, but this firestorm of need between them was – insanely – enough.

She opened her mouth to say something but could find no words to offer.

Instead, her hips moved from side to side and he laughed, a sound that invigorated her anger – but not enough. Sensual heat was drugging her.

"You cannot fight this, Sophia," he said quietly, reaching down and lifting her up, pushing her over his shoulder and curving a hand over her naked backside.

And he was right. Neither of them could. This need was as demanding of each of them.

Her stomach was in knots and her heart was squeezing painfully. She felt hot and cold and so desperately driven to this that she would have begged for him over and over and over if he'd asked it of her.

But she didn't need to.

He dropped her down onto the mattress and followed after, his powerful body so achingly familiar, so intensely *right*.

"You want to hate me, but you can't. At least, not all of me." And he thrust into her, his hard arousal taking fierce possession of her body.

She dug her nails into his back and heard herself groan, as pleasure rolled through her in addictive, insatiable waves, "Oh, go to hell!"

CHAPTER 11

"WHAT ARE YOU GOING to do?" She asked, sipping her coffee, her huge blue eyes fixing to him with a look of steel. It was hard to believe that twenty minutes ago they'd been wrapped in each other's arms, the madness of desire saturating them, cleaving them together.

She'd showered and pulled on a pale blue dress, styled her hair into a braid that wrapped around her head like a crown, and applied some gloss to her lips and mascara to lashes that were already so dark and long. She looked very beautiful, and completely untouchable.

And he wanted to touch her.

Though this was far from a conventional marriage, he understood now the tradition of a honeymoon. All he could think about was his wife, in his bed, beneath his body, calling his name into the sky... Perhaps they should have taken a month after the wedding. A month in bed, just her and him, sunshine, and sex on tap. Would that have cured him of this growing infatuation?

"To do?" He prompted, reaching for his own coffee and

taking a large gulp. It tasted of cinnamon and darkness. He drank it gratefully.

"The situation here. With Laith and Saliyah?"

His frown was reflexive. "It's complicated."

She pursed her lips. "So you've said." She leaned back a little in her chair, cradling her cup in her hands, her huge blue eyes probing his face. "She has to be allowed to go to university."

His eyes pierced Sophia's. "Why?"

"Education is a basic human right."

His nostrils flared. "You make it sound simple."

"It is simple."

"There is more than one girl's education at stake here."

"Yes, much more," she agreed, sipping her coffee. "If you prevent her from studying, you'll be saying you don't agree with me. That you think education should be unattainable for certain people in your country. You'll be condoning the servitude of a whole subset of this society."

He knew this to be true – the reality of that had been tormenting him for months. "And if I get involved," he said darkly, purely for the sake of argument, because it helped to have someone play the devil's advocate, "I'll be establishing a precedent that these tribes must yield to the palace. And I'd rather not do that."

"They are your subjects. Of course they must yield to you."

"There is a delicate balance," he insisted. "While in theory, yes, my rule is supreme, for decades we have existed in a kind of treatise state, a compromise – a balance. I do not wish to overrule Laith in this. I do not wish every single tribe to hear that I have taken that power from him – and for every single member of those tribes to realize their own rulers have no actual authority." He ground his teeth together.

Sophia scanned his face thoughtfully. "You want to maintain the status quo, but Malik, you are not just the king of the people who live in the cities and towns. These people *are* your subjects. They deserve your rights and protection. If Saliyah wants to study, that must be your priority."

Her words landed against his gut with a thud. "And what of these ancient, hallowed tribes, Sophia? Do I take steps that will see them eroded within my lifetime?"

"You don't know that will happen."

He arched a brow. "This is a hard life. A beautiful life, yes, but the danger of these tribes migrating closer to the cities is very real."

"This is not some tribe in the Andamans! They know there is a life out there, they see signs of it often enough. We came here by helicopter. You and I are both wearing watches, your guards carry guns and satellite phones. Their culture has already been diluted by the modern world."

"Isn't that even more reason to protect it? What if all of this is lost within a decade?"

"Then we'll cross that bridge when we get to it," she said with a wave of her hand. "Worrying about the future cannot change the present. You have a young woman who is exceptionally bright and who simply wants to learn. No future right can be earned by doing something wrong in the present. You cannot deny her the chance to study, Malik."

She had a way of speaking that made everything sound so easy, so reasonable, and yet it wasn't. He shook his head slowly, his eyes focused beyond her. "These tribes are an important part of our culture."

"Are they?" She crossed her legs beneath the table, her toes brushing his calf briefly. He felt impatience zip through him.

"It seems to me," she continued, without waiting for his

response, "that these tribes are a little like those beautiful, ancient tapestries that adorn the walls of the palace."

He waited for her to continue.

"I used to love looking at those tapestries. The first time I came here, I spent hours just staring, following the intricate threads, looking at them up close and imagining the long-ago hands that had knotted them together, forming patterns that, when you stood further back made the most amazing pictures. I would run my fingers over those threads –,"

"They are not to be touched," Malik said, but his lips were twitching into a smile of their own accord.

"So Addan told me," she laughed softly; his smile died. "He told me it was bad luck but I… it doesn't matter. My point is, they're incredibly beautiful and quite unique to this country. Nowhere in the world are there tapestries with those patterns and colours, the dyes they were able to produce a byproduct of the vegetables available only here." Her eyes widened. "These tribes are a part of your culture, but Malik, maybe they're also destined to become another part of your rich history. Maybe they won't survive the twenty first century. Societal change is a part of life. A hundred years ago, women in America couldn't vote, people from different cultures couldn't easily marry. Our world is always changing and evolving."

She reached across the table, curving her fingers over his, but he was finding it hard to hear her words over the pounding of his pulse through his body. Everything she said made sense, it was though she was drilling right into his brain and tapping on the knowledge he'd always held, but had been fighting hard to accept.

"Whether on your watch or our son or daughter's," she squeezed his hand, "or their child's or theirs, this way of life will survive or not. Laith has to make this workable for the younger people, so that they might choose to leave, and then come back. The tribes have to evolve in some small measure. That responsibility isn't yours to bear."

He let out a small sound of frustration. "This way of life is beautiful and valuable. It is unique and it must be protected."

She dipped her head forward. "But not by you."

He leaned forward a little, studying her face, her eyes that seemed to show him a whole galaxy in their depths. "By who then?"

"By Laith, by Saliyah, by the children out there who know only this reality." She expelled softly. "You have a role to play – and it is to speak for your people. *All* your people. Saliyah is counting on her King to protect her rights, to see that her life isn't diminished because she happened to have been born into this tribe. You cannot perform Laith's role, you cannot. Your responsibility here is clear cut."

He swallowed, her clarity something that sat within him like a piece of silver, shimmering and certain.

"You have tried to cajole Laith," she said quietly. "And if you do not act, you will be forcing a whole generation of people, this generation, to live without choices, without options. You will be enslaving them."

He dragged his palm over his chin, her words settling into his soul.

"He has forced you into making this ruling. It's regrettable, but you can't not protect her."

How often had he found himself butting against the idea of accepting her counsel? How often had he told himself she knew nothing of his people and their ways?

Too often.

Her insights were exactly what he needed to hear, and for a man who was used to relying purely on his own counsel, the realization that he'd enjoyed discussing this matter with his wife brought him very little pleasure.

———

She hadn't laughed so hard in a very long time.

"She's adorable," Sophia said, trying to emulate the tone of the dialect she'd been hearing that day.

'She' was a two year old girl with chubby legs, a rounded tummy and dark ringlets that sat close to her head like a little mop. Her eyes twinkled and her cheeks had dimples scored deep within them.

"She is trouble, more like," the little girl's mother responded, sitting down beside Sophia on a vibrant blue blanket. The little girl clapped her hands and danced some more, so Sophia laughed, and clapped along with her.

The little girl's mother put her finger out, touching Sophia's hand, tracing a line across her knuckles.

Sophia turned to face her.

"I have never seen skin like this," she said simply, smiling, her expression enigmatic. "You are like one of the ancient souls said to wander the desert."

Sophia laughed. "I have heard this before. Really, I'm not so pale, am I?"

"It is beautiful," the woman complimented. "Your highness."

She wanted to implore the woman to call her Sophia, but Malik had been right. She was the Sheikha, she also had a role to play.

"Thank you." She smiled though. "What is your name?"

"Fatima."

The little girl fell onto her bottom and for a moment, Sophia thought she might cry, but then she threw her head back and laughed and stamped her feet, before seeing a line of ants crawling past and stopping to investigate them.

Sophia could have watched her all day – she had been watching her for the better part of an hour.

It was hot, but she'd become a little more used to it, and one of the tribeswomen had provided her with a fan of sorts, made of lace and delicate branches, just the slightest movement circulated air around her face.

"She is like my *shabat*," Fatima said. "My grandfather."

Something spiked in Sophia – a curiosity. Would their child be like her? Her mother or her father? Her heart squeezed. Or like Malik?

"It must be lovely to see traces of someone you love in your daughter," Sophia murmured, as the little girl stood up on those impossibly sweet little legs and tottered towards Sophia.

"It is the way of life, is it not? The continuity of things."

Sophia's chest was weighted by grief. Not all things continued. She thought of her father and Addan, and sadness was pervasive.

But that was all the more reason to persist with this – to ensure she fell pregnant. Life was the only antidote to death. All those people would live on in their child, in some way. Perhaps it would be a little girl with fire in her soul, like her sister Arabella, and a kind heart like Addan, and a love of games and Christmas, like her father.

Their child would give life back to those who had lost it.

"Yes," Sophia whispered, turning to Fatima and smiling wistfully.

"You have a baby," Fatima asked.

Sophia shook her head. "No, not yet."

"I think you do," Fatima corrected, and Sophia realized it hadn't been a question at all, so much as a statement.

"Oh, no," Sophia shook her head.

But Fatima reached across and put a hand on Sophia's belly, closed her eyes and inhaled deeply.

Sophia felt light-headed and strong, all at once. A rush of

cold air seemed to pass through her, and she saw pink lights glistening beneath her eyelids.

"Yes," Fatima murmured, moving her hand slightly. "There is a powerful life inside you, your highness." She moved her other hand to Sophia's belly, hovering it slightly above the skin. "Very powerful indeed." And then, she opened her eyes, pulled her hands away and smiled. "You have my congratulations and my sympathy," she said from the corner of her mouth.

"Sympathy?"

"As the mother of one incredibly strong-willed child, power is not always a good thing."

Sophia sucked in a deep breath, the words impossible to make sense of. "I'm not pregnant."

Fatima tilted her head to face Sophia's. "I beg to differ. Your highness."

Fatima's eyes ran over Sophia's face. "This is not the news you were expecting?"

"I … wasn't expecting any news," she said weakly. "I … we've only been married a few weeks."

Fatima's eyes grew watchful. "Which makes even more sense," Fatima nodded. "This little soul wants very much to be here." She nodded towards Sophia's stomach. "There is a power in that child. I think it is desperate to be a part of this life, of your family."

Sophia's heart turned over. She wanted to beg Fatima to stop talking like this, because suddenly, all of her dreams were coming true, and she wasn't sure how she could bear it.

Her family.

She swallowed, and unconsciously, her eyes lifted to the tent which housed Malik. He'd been locked in consultation with Laith for much of the day.

"How can you tell?" She asked, focusing on the science – or lack thereof – of this diagnosis.

Fatima frowned slightly. "I'm a seer."

"A seer?" Sophia's heart sank. "Like a future-teller?"

"No," Fatima shook her head slightly. "More like what you would call a doctor. I can see, or feel, perhaps more accurately, what is happening inside a person." She touched Sophia's stomach once more. "It is a gift. My family has possessed it for generations. It is, perhaps, most powerful in her." She jerked her head towards her daughter.

"And is it... accurate?"

Fatima's expression showed amusement. "You are skeptical."

"I'm sorry. I don't mean to be. It's just..."

"You are from out there," Fatima gestured with her palm heavenward, towards the outside world. "You rely on things like this," she moved her hand to Sophia's watch. "And have forgotten the senses we all possess."

"Perhaps," Sophia responded noncommittally, disappointment surging. For a brief moment, she'd truly believed she might be pregnant. But how absurd, to get swept up in some kind of witchcraft.

"Close your eyes a moment," Fatima suggested.

Sophia wasn't sure she wanted to, and yet, she was fascinated by this. At least, fascinated by what Fatima was saying, if not convinced of there being any truth to it. She blinked her eyes shut.

"Hold your hands here," Fatima said, taking Sophia's hands and arranging them palm up on her knees.

Sophia opened her eyes to find Fatima watching her carefully.

"Keep them shut," she smiled.

Sophia laughed apologetically. "I'm sorry."

"You are a curious person. I understand. Close them."

Sophia did as she'd been told, sweeping her eyes shut.

"Feel this," Fatima murmured.

At first, Sophia felt nothing. Just hot, from the sun, from the day that surrounded them. But then, something began to spark in her fingertips, and a different heat, more of a gentle warmth, seemed to throb in her veins.

Her breath grew rhythmic and she saw a flash of green behind her eyes. She kept them shut.

"You are sad," Fatima said, after several moments, and the warmth migrated higher, to Sophia's chest.

She swallowed.

"A deep sadness, right here." And now she pressed a finger to Sophia's chest and she felt that grief – some very old, some very new – spiral through her. "You must allow yourself to feel it. Accept that it is a part of who you are. Sadness like this never goes away – it is like a stone in the desert, covered over by sand but always there, deep inside."

Sophia swallowed. Her heart tugged painfully.

There was a noise. Sophia blinked her eyes open and the world seemed to tip completely off its axis. Fatima smiled. Behind her, the children were playing, running in circles, each trying to catch one another.

"Do you believe now?"

Sophia's heart lurched. Did she? She couldn't say for certain.

She watched the children play and a servant brought iced tea and vine leaves wrapped around rice and dates. She ate with the women of the tribe, and found herself laughing even more.

And as the day moved towards afternoon, something settled inside her soul.

A certainty that Malik's fears were unfounded. This way of life wouldn't disintegrate so easily. There was magic here, and love. It was impossible to imagine that all of these people would turn their backs on this life they knew.

Before dusk, with no sight of Malik, Sophia settled the

younger children of the village into a circle, and she began to tell them a story – one of the ancient tales Sheikh Bashira had taught her, when she was just a little girl. She had read the books so many times over the years, she knew the tales by heart. She spoke slowly, conscious there was a difference in the Abu Fayan she spoke and the dialect of this tribe. But it was close enough. Close enough for the children's faces to sparkle with wonderment as she spoke of ancient traders and the monsters that pursued them across these deserts, the caves that shielded them with their magic and art. She saw the way they laughed at the antics of Jaffaran, the ancient King who was so very vain that he insisted on anyone who saw him knowing how rich and important he was. So much so that he went into the Ocean of Alindor wearing all of his jewels and crowns, and sank to the bottom of the sea.

She lowered her voice to a whisper and spoke of the pirates who had hunted for those jewels and been taken by the sea as well, swallowed up into its deep belly – a reminder that seeking earthly wealth is beneath us, and can only lead to danger.

She saw their faces light up and the seed of hope that Fatima had planted in her belly exploded into an orchard.

Was it possible that a child, just as sweet as these little ones, might be growing in her already?

HE KNEW the story of Jaffaran well. It had been one of his father's favourites to recount. Sheikh Bashira had known the danger of pursuing personal wealth in place of prioritizing the people.

He knew the story well and yet he'd never heard it told like this.

He stood on the edge of the group, outside of his wife's

field of vision, and he listened as she spoke, the words flowing from her lips almost as if by magic.

He stood behind her and saw the rapt expressions of the tribe's children, the smiles of the adults who were gathering to hear their Sheikha, and pride burst through him.

It was ridiculous and misplaced. Not only had he not chosen her as his wife, he'd made it clear he didn't relish the prospect of her holding any such position. And yet his father had been right. His brother had been right.

Sophia was perfect for this. *We all have our roles to play*, she'd said. And she was playing hers with absolute perfection. He had no idea what else she might have been destined for, what other life may have called her had Bashira and her father not been friends, had Bashira not decided that Sophia had a place within the palace. But he had, and he had chosen well.

Malik had been the last to realize that.

Much later, as the helicopter lifted up out of the desert, and the tribe stood below, waving their farewell, Sophia pressed her forehead to the window, staring down at them, and Malik watched her.

"They're beautiful," she said, her admiration apparent in the tone of her voice. "I didn't expect to be so touched."

"Their way of life is unique," he agreed.

"What did you decide with Laith?"

Malik expelled a long breath. "He is going to permit Saliyah to leave." His smile was grim. "With his blessing, and that of the tribe. But privately, he is going to beg her to return when she has completed her studies."

Sophia tilted her head. "Do you think she will?"

Malik was quiet on that score. He had his doubts. "I hope so."

Sophia tilted her head in agreement, then turned away from him a moment. When she spoke, he could hear her courtesy of the headsets they both wore. "I met an interesting woman today. Fatima."

"Ah. The tribe's *naraan*. Their Seer."

"Yes, she told me." Sophia cleared her throat. She seemed hesitant – unusual for her. "Do you believe in that stuff?"

"Yes."

Her surprise was obvious.

"But it's kind of voodoo, don't you think?"

"I think not knowing how something works doesn't invalidate it," he corrected.

"So if you were unwell, would you go to her?"

He leaned back in his seat, focusing straight ahead. "When Laith's grandson was four years old, he became very tired. It happened fast. Within weeks. At first they thought it was a fever. Or that he'd eaten something which did not agree with him. But Fatima knew. From the start, she said something was different in his blood; it had changed its rhythm. It felt thick and discordant with his body."

Sophia's heart turned over. "And?"

"He had leukemia." Malik turned to face Sophia. "Laith sent him to the city for treatment and he is now a healthy eight year old."

"I met him today," Sophia murmured softly, something like excitement in her voice.

"I have no idea how it works, but yes, Sophia, I believe Fatima's family has this ability, much like some people can divine the source of water, far beneath the surface. It is one of the many things I seek to protect, when I talk about preserving this way of life."

But Sophia no longer seemed to be listening.

CHAPTER 12

"I HAVE A MEETING," he said, as the helicopter came over the palace. "Hereth messaged while we were out there. I'll be a while."

Sophia nodded, but she was distracted. All she could think about was Fatima, and her insistence that Sophia was pregnant.

But Malik was intent. He reached across, putting a hand on Sophia's knee. "You will move to my room."

The words were spoken as an order, but she felt the hint of a question there. The helicopter dropped lower, closer to the palace. Dusk was drawing in. The sight was incredible.

"Sophia?"

She hadn't planned to keep her own rooms once they were married. It had just happened that way.

She opened her mouth to agree, but he spoke first.

"I will have your rooms locked up if you do not say 'yes'," he muttered, and she jerked her eyes to his. She should have been annoyed, but she wasn't. He was half-joking, but she heard the madness in his voice, the sound of desperation and her heart turned over. He wanted her with him.

But just in his bed?

Probably.

She didn't know how she felt about that – not good. And yet, his desperate, aching need filled her with a fierce glow of possession.

"That won't be necessary, your highness," she murmured.

Victory flashed in the depths of his eyes.

"I'll be late. But you'll be there?"

It was a simple question yes it didn't feel so completely simple to answer. She nodded, slowly, and it was like she was sealing her fate in some vital way – more so than when they'd said their vows.

The helicopter touched down and the rotor blades began to slow.

He leaned forward, to get a better view through the window. His aids were approaching. Some other urgent matter apparently called him.

He turned to her and lifted off the headset, his palm brushing her cheek for a brief moment, sending goose bumps down her spine. It was an accidental touch. He removed his own headset but then looked at her, his eyes boring directly into hers.

"I didn't want your help, Sophia. I resented your offer. But your counsel, in the desert, was... it was what I needed to hear." A muscle jerked in his jaw and he looked away for a moment, giving her stunned heart a moment to recover. "You said exactly what Addan would have said, had he lived."

She swallowed, her eyes unconsciously reflecting the complexity of that compliment. "We spoke often. I suppose much of my opinion is informed by him."

Malik's smile was grim. "Undoubtedly."

The door was opened and Malik stepped out of the helicopter, waiting with a hand held up for her. She sucked in a fortifying breath, her emotions tumbling all over themselves, and then she moved. She put her hand in his, and a bolt of electricity slammed up her sides. She jerked her eyes to his; had he felt it?

It was impossible to tell.

He was the exalted ruler Sheikh Malik bin Hazari again, the man who'd just thanked her for her advice nowhere in evidence. He waited for her, walking beside her to the palace, but his attention was held by Minister Hereth as he went, and as they swept inside, he paused for the briefest of moments to fix her with an intent look.

"Tonight," he said, scanning her face, as though she might have changed her mind between the helicopter arrival and now.

She nodded.

He spun on his heel and moved down the corridor, the robes he'd worn in the desert flying behind him, loose and spectacular. Surrounded by other men, she couldn't help but see how different he was. How much bigger, stronger, how much more regal and masculine.

He was spectacular.

She stood there, staring at him, for several long moments, until he reached the end of the corridor and turned from view.

It was only then that she realized her heart was racing.

She ate alone and picked up a book – one of her favourites. She'd lost count of how many times she'd read it – The Republic, by Plato. She turned to the frontispiece and read the inscription from Addan.

'THE BEGINNING IS *the most important part of the work.' And now is our beginning.*

Rex.

SHE RAN her finger over his bold, confident writing and swept her eyes shut. He'd given it to her for her seventeenth birthday.

God, she'd been such a child! It had been the night he'd told her of their parents' wishes, the night he'd asked if she would like to take up her place at his side, as his Sheikha. They'd dined with his family afterwards, and Malik had gone to no effort to hide his disapproval of the betrothal. He'd left almost as soon as dinner was finished, and not come back for months.

Looking back, their betrothal was as unromantic and business-like as it got – and that befit what they were to one another. Dear, dear friends. Their engagement had been sensible. Reasonable. Measured.

Everything about her friendship with Addan had been smooth seas for as far as the eye could see. They'd never argued. *Never.* There'd been no passion between them. Had she thought it would grow? Or did she not care that it was absent?

It was so hard to know now.

Certainly, she'd loved him. Oh, she'd loved him with all of herself, but not in the way a woman loved her husband.

She swallowed, her mind pulling her toward Malik, her pulse picking up, racing harder, faster. There were a thousand words she could use to describe what she felt for Malik, but not one of them fit perfectly. It wasn't easy and smooth sailing as it had been with Addan. It was the exact opposite. She lusted after him, absolutely. She desired him, completely. But it was more complex than that.

She… craved him. Not just his body. His presence. When he was with her, looking at her, talking to her, when they were in the same room together, she felt like she was vibrating on a wholly new frequency.

She felt… everything.

Her stomach swooped like she'd dived out of an airplane, and she blinked her eyes shut, trying to bring order to her chaotic thoughts.

She didn't love her husband. She couldn't. They were so different. He was *nothing* like Addan, and she *had* loved Addan, yet it hadn't been like this. Not even a little. She couldn't begin to compare the way she felt for the two brothers.

Unconsciously, her hand curved over her stomach and she wondered at what Fatima had felt there. Was it possible there was a child growing inside of her?

She'd been dubious, but something *felt* different.

And the idea of having Malik's baby made her heart soar. She smiled unconsciously, her head spinning, her eyes wandering to the watch she wore, checking the time frequently.

She turned the first page with exasperation, needing a distraction, and read the opening, her mind absorbing the words even as all of her was attuned to the palace and its sounds. An hour or so later, she stood, moving to the balcony, bringing the book with her. The night was dark and still, no hint of the desert breezes to bring relief. She stared up at the constellations, stars that were so different to what she'd grown up with, stars that were shimmering and beautiful, with their pulsing lights against the ink black of the night sky.

She breathed in, and ran her hand over her stomach again.

What had Fatima said? Something about the continuity of things, and this baby would indeed be that. Their loved ones were out there, up in heaven, looking down on them, and through this baby, they'd be brought back to life in some way.

Whenever she and Malik had a baby, even if she weren't pregnant now, that baby would grow up hearing stories of his uncle Addan, his grandfathers, all the people who would have loved that baby to bits and who weren't here to do so.

She continued reading, her eyes growing heavy as she reached the halfway point of the book.

She stood, making a cup of spice tea, and taking it to the bed. She lay down, reading, sipping tea, and within a few minutes her eyes grew heavier still and she fell asleep, the book open on the pillow beside her.

IT WAS the soonest he could get away. He worked through the afternoon and evening, eating *amashyr* for dinner, something simple he could manage with his hands alone, dealing with the matters that had arisen in his absence. And finally, a minute before midnight, he closed his laptop, pushed back from his desk and addressed the staff who were working around him.

"That's enough for now. Go. We can resume in the morning."

And he'd walked out without waiting for a response.

As he neared his suite of rooms, he felt like a spring was coiling tighter and tighter inside of him. Only a few paces from the enormous doors that heralded the entrance to his room, he understood why.

Despite what she'd said, he had no idea, he couldn't have known with any certainty that he'd find her sitting there waiting for him, or not.

And if she wasn't?

He braced himself on the exterior to his apartment,

uncaring – barely noticing – the guards who stood sentinel on either side.

If she wasn't?

An image came to him out of nowhere, of him going into her room, lifting her sleeping body over his shoulder and carrying her to his room. Of having her suite locked up for good.

A muscle jerked in his cheek because he knew, beyond a shadow of a doubt, that he was capable of such an act. He knew that his need to have her within reach every night was primal and physical and absolute, and that he would do just about anything to achieve it.

But the part of him that wasn't a beast, that wasn't an animal acting on instincts, the part of him that was educated and had at least a degree of civility, knew forcing her into his suite of rooms wasn't the answer. He wouldn't – couldn't – do that.

Not to any woman, but especially not to the woman who – were it not for a twist of fate – would have been married to his brother.

He stifled a groan and pushed the doors open impatiently, sweeping into his rooms and looking around. Darkness surrounded him, but there was the hint of a glow coming from his bedroom.

Hope surged in his chest. He strode through, the tension in his body growing with every step.

He paused inside the door jamb, and simply stared.

She was beautiful – always beautiful. But asleep like this, she looked so young and so fragile. Awake, she was feisty, combative, sweet, smart – she was so vibrant. But asleep?

Something pulled inside of him.

Something dark.

Something that troubled him.

Something that reminded him of that night he'd taken his

stallion and run, fast, to the caves near the Oasis of *Manama*. A doubt, an uncertainty, and an ache.

He looked at her and remembered her as she'd been then. Remembered how he'd felt when he'd first seen her.

And he remembered every reason he'd had for keeping her at a distance all these years.

He circumnavigated the bed, moving to his side, picking up the book she'd been reading absentmindedly, and smiling to himself when he saw what it was.

The Republic had been one of his favourites. As a child, their mother had read it to them, both Malik and Addan adoring the wisdom, feeling its relevance and insight. Her own cover was well-worn, as though she read it often.

He turned to the front page, and saw the hint of scribble through it.

At his brother's familiar hand, he stilled.

Addan.

Addan had given this book to her.

It was yet another thing she shared with his brother – because she was his. She always would be. She was an inherited bride, a borrowed wife.

She wanted them to be 'friends', but that had never been enough for him.

With a sinking heart, he moved towards the bathroom, stripping naked and starting the shower running.

He stood under the water for a long time, his mind working double-time, trying to make sense of the fact that he was married to the woman who had been hand-picked to marry his brother.

Trying to make sense of any of it – and failing.

SHE REACHED for him on autopilot, somewhere in the very middle hours of the night, when dawn was still a long way off and the night's magic was at its thickest. She reached for him from the depths of her sleep, her hands finding his chest, running over his muscles, her fingers seeking every ridge and curve, her palms flat against his muscular abdomen. Lower, to the curve of his rear.

"Sophia," he murmured, low and throaty, his eyes firing open, pinning her with the strength of their inquisition.

She didn't say anything, at first. She pushed up, straddling him, her long hair falling over her shoulders in curtains. "You didn't wake me," she said quietly, dropping her mouth, kissing him, tasting him.

He groaned. "No."

She reached for the hem of her nightgown and lifted it, casting it across the room, and he sat up, bringing his mouth to her breasts, flicking her nipples with his tongue until she was incandescent with desire.

"Please," she groaned, lifting up so his hands could slip inside the elastic of her underpants and push them down. She stepped out of them, bringing her body back over his, craving him, needing him, every ounce of her aching for him. She took him deep inside, and he thrust his hips, so she arched her back, her body falling apart, desire like a firework in her gut.

She dug her nails into his shoulder and he pulled up, kissing her again, kissing her breasts, her mouth, her throat, sucking on her flesh and gripping her hips so hard and with all the desperation he felt – that was deep inside her too.

Their explosion was quick and simultaneous. Holding one another tight, they tipped over the edge, with the evening's magic thick around them, the heat of the day nothing compared to the fire they generated.

Her breathing was raspy, her skin covered in perspiration, her heart racing. She looked down at him, and her heart skipped a beat. Because there was something in his expression she hadn't expected. Something she couldn't make sense of, that filled her with a sense of apprehension.

It was compounded when he shifted his weight, gently tumbling her onto the bed beside him. He pulled the cotton sheet up, laying it gently over her shoulders.

"Go to sleep, Sheikha."

DAWN YOKED SLOWLY over the desert, passing gold and violet hues over the palace. She looked out at it, her eyes watching the changes in colour, the gradual bringing of light, and she thought of his tattoo. She thought of the idea behind it, of light coming after dark. That even the worst storms lead to a clearing, eventually.

But when you were in the middle of a storm, how could you find the light?

She rolled over gently; he was facing her, his eyes shut.

She stared at him, her heart beating faster, harder, and she knew where the light was. She knew where it had always been.

Love.

She loved him.

Her breath caught in her throat as she turned that idea over, and it was like every single piece of a puzzle was clicking instantly into place. She felt it with a visceral, absolute truth.

She loved him.

He was her husband, and circumstance alone had led to their marriage. She'd never expected to feel anything for him but desire – a desire she'd become adept at concealing. She hadn't expected to find him captivating and enchanting and enigmatic. She hadn't expected to hear the struggles he dealt with and to want to reach out and wrest those troubles from his shoulders. She hadn't expected to want to sleep with him and wake up with him, to *be* with him, always.

She reached out, a smile on her lips as she pressed a finger to his nose. He lifted his hand, swatting hers away, before opening his eyes with confusion. Confusion gave way to something else. A smile hinted at his lips before it was flattened.

"Sophia."

"Uh huh."

Silence. But a silence that crackled with words not spoken. And suddenly, her conversation with Fatima sat inside her like a butterfly's chrysalis on the day of emergence. She felt it weakening and giving way and she bit down on her lip, to hold it steady for a moment or two, and then, she cleared her throat. His eyes latched to hers.

"Fatima said," she whispered, so softly the words were barely audible. "That is to say, Fatima believes me to be pregnant."

The words flooded the room, quiet, but with the power of a thousand drums.

His eyes widened, and he was very, very still, watching her while his own expression was impossible to interpret. "Does she?"

The question was flattened of any emotion.

That poked a hole in Sophia's happiness, but only for a moment. "I mean, she might be wrong, but … you said she's got this talent and the moment she said it, I felt… is it ridiculous to say I felt different?"

Malik didn't respond.

She swallowed, waiting. "I know I'll have to do a test. I meant to ask Awan to organise something for me yesterday but I … didn't. I can do one today, so we're sure."

"Yes," he frowned. "I will organise the chief of medicine to attend to you." He turned away from her, reaching for the phone on his side of the bed. He spoke into it in rapid-fire Abu Fayan and then stood, reaching for a pair of pants. She watched as he pulled them up, over his cock, covering his body, and confusion spun inside of her.

"The doctor will be here within minutes."

"I don't need a doctor, Malik. Just a pregnancy test. I can get one brought from a pharmacy."

"A doctor will be better able to confirm at this early stage, no?"

He was right. It made sense. Only her anxieties had nothing to do with the possible appearance of a doctor. "Malik? You're not... happy?"

His frown deepened. "We don't know for sure that there is anything to be happy about yet."

"But... I mean... you want a baby. You're desperate for us to have a child, so you have your heir. Isn't it a good thing if this has happened so quickly?"

His eyes met hers, and there was a challenge in them she couldn't comprehend. "Yes, Sophia. It would be a very good thing."

CHAPTER 13

S HE WAS PREGNANT, CONFIRMED by a blood test. The results had been expedited and the doctor surprised by the increased level of her hormones, given the earliness of the baby's gestation.

'A strong pregnancy!' The chief physician had concluded, and Malik told himself he was glad. It was essential for the country and the kingdom. And yet, he also knew it spelled an end for them. He couldn't keep having sex with the woman his brother had intended to marry, not when the sole purpose of this marriage was procreation.

They'd done what they set out to achieve.

It was over.

Finished.

Despite what she might have said she wanted, he knew Addan had been the man she loved, the man she'd chosen. Malik was tormented by imaginings of what Sophia's life *should* have been, married to Addan, happy, laughing, relaxed. His gut tightened every time he imagined that, imagined seeing her as his sister-in-law, at government events, so beautiful and... content... on Addan's arm.

He was tormented by what should have been – and what was.

Malik worked late into the night, every night for seven nights after the discovery of her condition. He worked late, even when it wasn't necessary. And when he didn't work, he sat in his office, acknowledging he was hiding from this, from her.

After two weeks, despite the lateness of his arrival in his suite of rooms, Sophia was awake.

His first thought, when he entered the apartment and saw her pacing from one side to the other, her skin so pale, her expression serious, was that something was wrong.

"What is it?" Urgency propelled him across the room, his dark eyes rushing over her. "Are you okay?"

"No." A simple response. "I'm not fine. Malik, what's going on?"

Caution overtook concern. "What do you mean?"

"I've barely seen you in a fortnight, ever since the doctor came and confirmed the pregnancy." She frowned, and she looked so vulnerable in that moment, so frail and small, his chest thumped. How in the world could she carry his child?

He remembered how she'd been in that moment, her expression showing him everything she'd felt. Her happiness. Her relief. Her gladness. It had been like a sledgehammer in his gut. Where he felt only disappointment that it was the ending of their togetherness, her relief had been palpable.

"I thought you wanted this," she said, quietly.

"I do."

She shook her head. "But you don't. You're… annoyed. Angry? I can't work it out. I thought the whole point of this marriage was to get you an heir…"

"It was." His eyes narrowed, as the simplicity of this situation revealed itself to him. "And now we've done that. You're pregnant."

Comprehension dawned. He saw the way her brow furrowed and then shifted, her eyes jerking to his and then away. She spun from him, moving towards the balcony, but not stepping out onto it. "So that's it," she said thickly. "I'm pregnant and you don't want to be with me anymore?"

He expelled a sigh of frustration. "You just said it yourself, having a child is the sole purpose of this union."

She nodded, but it was just a jerk of her head. "So you don't want me at all, on any level?" She prompted, turning to face him, lifting a hand to his chest. Of course, she must feel the racing of his heart; that must answer her questions.

His eyes hooked to hers. "I want you to be happy," he said, finally, after a long pause.

"But our marriage really is just a sham, right? You've got me pregnant and now you're done with me? So what, Malik, do you go back to having sex with other women? Sleeping your way around Europe, and I turn a blind eye?"

His gut rolled at the idea.

"Until a year or two passes and we need to have another child? Is that the marriage you envisage for us?"

He shook his head, reaching out and gripping her shoulders, pulling her body closer to his, so close that he wondered at his restraint in not kissing her.

"I promise you here and now, *Sharafaha*, I will not sleep with another woman so long as we are married."

She stared up at him, her eyes huge in her delicate face. "So you're going to abstain from sex altogether?" Her eyes lowered. "I thought…"

"What did you think?" A gravelled request.

"I thought you really wanted me." She swallowed, her throat moving visibly with the movement. "I thought you wanted me as much as I want you."

He dropped his hands to his side, seared by her words. "You were not wrong."

Emboldened, she closed the small gap between them, lifting her hands to his chest. "Then why are you freezing me out like this, Malik?"

He looked away from her, his chest contorting with the force of his feelings. "What choice do I have?"

She pulled a face. "What's that supposed to mean? I'm your wife…"

"Yes, you're my wife," he spat, moving away from her, stalking across the room and pouring himself a measure of whisky. "You're the wife I stole from my dead brother. The woman who should have been his, who should, right now, be growing his baby in her belly. You're the woman I've spent more than a decade ignoring." He threw the drink back angrily, his expression tense.

"What do you want from me, *Sharafaha*? Do you want me to pretend any of this is real? Do you want me to act like I don't know how little this was either of our first choice? You should be married to him! If he hadn't died, you'd be his wife now, my sister-in-law. Instead, this is our life, you're my wife and I'm your husband, and we're having a child together, but I'm not going to pretend…"

"I'm not asking you to pretend," she cut into his monologue, her expression pinched, her eyes showing her hurt. "I'm asking you to accept that there's something real between us."

His eyes latched to hers and the world opened up, swallowing him into the depths of its fiery belly.

"Something real?" He repeated, his voice deep, the words thick.

"Yes, damn it!" She glared at him, closing the distance. "You're not Addan, and this isn't the marriage I had planned for. But that doesn't mean what we have isn't good, and isn't… enough, on its own."

"Don't." He cut her off, the word like ice. "Don't do this."

"Do what?" She demanded. "I've lost too much in my life not to fight for what matters, Malik."

"To fight for what?" His eyes narrowed, his expression like steel. "Were it not for his death, you would be my brother's wife. Every time I have touched you, every time I have wanted you, do you not think I knew how wrong it was? Do you not think I felt that betrayal? He has been deprived of so much. He should be King, not me! He should be right here, watching this new life grow inside of you, feeling elated at the prospect of becoming a father. He should be here!"

"Yes," she whispered, curving her hands over her stomach, her eyes clouding with grief. "I know that."

"And if he were," Malik continued, "You would be happily, blissfully married to him. You would be happy."

"I am happy. I think we could be happy together."

"I saw you with him," Malik snapped. "I know what it looks like when you are happy, and it is not this. You *desire* me. Our bodies are like fire together. That is all. And it is not enough to make a marriage – not the kind of marriage you want."

"Because you're fighting me all the time," she stamped her foot onto the tiled floor. "You and I are great together, but every time we get close, you shut me out again. You refuse to let me in. What are you so afraid of? Don't you think you deserve to be happy?"

He swore under his breath and pulled her into his arms, bringing her against his body. "I can't be happy with you, *Sharafaha*. Circumstances make it impossible. The more I want you, the more guilt I feel. You are in my blood and my mind and yet I can't see you without seeing you with him – without seeing the pair of you. And I resent him, Sophia, my own brother, because if he were here – alive and breathing right now – you would have chosen him. You *did* choose him."

"He was chosen for me," she said softly, his words making her spirit stumble a little.

"That's irrelevant. Given the choice between him and me, you would have always chosen him, wouldn't you?"

She was so quiet, so still, as if frozen in time, torn between love, loyalty and this life she found herself in.

"Don't answer," he growled, giving her a reprieve. "We both know the answer. Addan is the man you want, the man you love, the man you wish you could be with even now. I commend you for how hard you're trying with me, but there's no point carrying on with this charade. We married for this purpose and having achieved it, we can dispense with the pretence and go back to our own lives."

"I loved Addan," she whispered, turning away from him, swallowing once more, moving towards the edge of the bed and sitting down on it. "I adored him." Salty tears threatened to fill her eyes. She blinked, focussing on her brightly coloured toe nails. "There isn't a day that goes by when I don't think of him, when I don't miss him. When I don't re-read the hundreds of letters he sent me, laugh at them and cry, wishing he were here."

Malik's gut twisted, her words only serving to confirm what he already knew, but oh, how they hurt. "And I am sorry for you, that he died and you were forced into this marriage, with me."

"Stop it," she muttered. "Stop."

"What? Being honest? Do you not think it is time for us to have this conversation?"

"Do you think anyone could force me into marriage?" She glared at him. "Do you think I would have done this if I didn't know it to be right?"

"Right for who, Sophia?"

She shook her head. "For you, for me, for this country…"

"No." The word crushing. "Nothing about this is

right, and it never has been. It's madness. I should have forced parliament to revoke your marriage contract, to free you from this obligation."

"But you didn't," her eyes were filled with an emotion he interpreted as hope and it crushed him to see it there. How could she have hope after all they'd been through?

"No." He crossed his arms over his broad chest. "Damn it, I believed we could do this and that it wouldn't matter that he had loved you with all his heart. I believed I would forget that you and my brother were a pair for as long as you knew one another."

"Yes." Her eyes swept shut for a moment as she appeared to work to steady her breath. "We were. And let me say this: I loved Addan. He was everything to me." She fixed him with a cool stare, but it was a counterfeit. He could see the fine tremble of her limbs, the pout of her lips, the flush of pink on her skin. "I hardly knew you – you went out of your way to avoid me and I have always been glad, because there was something about you that knocked me completely off-kilter whenever you were nearby. I thought it was dislike but now that I've been with you, I see it so much more clearly. Addan was my best friend, but I have wanted you almost as long as I've known you, Malik. As a girl, how could I understand what this meant? When you came to Addan's birthday with that beautiful supermodel, I thought I was *annoyed* at you. I thought I didn't *like* you. But I wanted to claw her eyes out. I looked at the way you were holding her, at the way she touched you, and I ached to feel that, to be in your arms."

She lifted her eyes to his, and he stood completely still, refusing to believe her, refusing to let her words answer the needs buried deep within him. "*This* is real, between us."

He couldn't let her words soothe him: he couldn't allow that to be their truth. "Yet if he'd lived, you would never have acted on that. How can I relish my wife's desire for me, knowing it is because of my brother's death?"

"I don't know," she whispered honestly, because that same question was in her own mind. "Except, you have to try. We both loved Addan; neither of us will ever forget him. But he's dead, and he wouldn't want you to live in some kind of self-punishing purgatory for the rest of your life. We're married now - it's you and me - and we're going to be parents."

Those words pulled at him, offering pleasure and pride when he wanted to feel only duty.

"I want you, Malik. I want you in this bed, making love to me; it's the only thing here that makes sense. I want you to stop fighting me all the time and start fighting for the life we could share."

Her words battered his insides. He heard them and tried to listen to them, but always, he saw Addan, he saw his brother's mangled body contrasted to his happy face when he'd spoken of Sophia, and he knew she would *always* belong to Addan. That she *should* always belong to Addan. Even when they felt like they were moving forward, it wasn't fair and it wasn't right.

"No." He pulled himself up to his full height. "You were Addan's fiancé. You have always been his, *Sharafaha,* from the first moment you arrived in this country and you stared at him as though he was a piece of you that had been missing all your life. You have always been his and you always will be."

She let out a small sob, but he didn't look at her.

"Why can't I be yours as well?" The question was so soft, he didn't hear it at first. And then, it slammed through him with the force of a thousand dam walls bursting, drenching him with the tsunami of her expectations, of the life she was suggesting for them.

"Because I don't want that." The words ripped him to pieces, and he saw for himself the effect they had on Sophia.

He told himself he was glad – if he had to be brutal to get her to understand how he felt then so be it, but watching her crumple like this, watching her strength be battered from the inside out, made his gut clench painfully.

Only, he had to make her understand. Wanting her, choosing to make this marriage real, would mean being glad Addan was dead, and he could never let himself feel that.

He spun away from her, ignoring her pain, shutting her out, just like she'd accused him of.

"If you'd prefer to move back to your suite of rooms, I'll understand." The words were cold, as though he didn't particularly care either way. Then, he swept out of his apartment with no idea of where the hell he was going to go – certain only that he had to get the hell away from all of this as soon as he could.

ONLY SOPHIA HAD ALWAYS BEEN a fighter, and she followed him. Not immediately. It took her a minute or two to pull herself together, to stop tears from falling down her cheeks, but then, she wrapped a robe around herself quickly and moved out of his suite.

She couldn't have said what drove her, and why. She moved through the palace on instinct, through the ancient corridors, down the wide marble staircase, and out into the garden that ran towards the desert. She breathed in the acrid sand-filled air, and stared up at the stars, and then she heard it.

A horse.

She turned in time to catch a glimpse of her husband – unmistakably him – mounted on the back of the incredible beast, riding hard and fast.

Without thinking, without preparing, she called out, as loud as she could, "Malik!"

At first, there was nothing, then the horse slowed, the silhouette of darkness she could see, anyway, and began to move towards the palace once more. It took the scrambling steps out of the desert as though they were nothing until Malik was above her, his eyes staring down at her, his expression grim, even in this fine sliver of moonlight.

"Don't run away," she said simply. "Don't tell me to move out of your rooms. Don't just shut me out."

He lifted his head, looking towards the horizon. "I had no idea what marriage to you would be like," he said, finally. "I considered it my duty to marry you, and to take you to bed."

Heat stirred inside of her.

"I thought I would take little pleasure in it. I presumed it would be perfunctory and dull. I imagined our marriage would be a minor inconvenience I would generally ignore. I had no idea," he stared at her, "that you would find a way into my blood. That I would want you to beg for me in my bed over and over as a way of knowing it was *me* you wanted. I had no idea how much I would want to triumph over my brother in this regard, nor how that petty need would tear me up."

She swallowed, lifting a hand to the horse's neck, but the horse made a cranky noise and stepped backwards. Apparently the beautiful beast had picked up the emotional discord between Sophia and his master.

"I need to go."

"Like when you were a teenager and you would run to the desert?" She snapped. "You're a grown man, and a Sheikh. You cannot run from your responsibilities –,"

He held up a hand to silence her. "My responsibilities go with me, wherever I travel." He kicked the horse's sides and the animal backed up further.

"Stay here," she said angrily. "Stay here and fight for this, Malik. We can make this work."

His eyes glittered like dark gems in the night sky. "No, *sharafaha*. We can't."

───────

SHE HELD her arms to the side with an air of patience that hid the state of suspension her heart had been dropped into. She kept a polite smile on her face when her insides were twisting and tormented by grief and absence.

In the month since they'd argued in the gardens, that moonlit night, she'd seen her husband three times, all at official events.

At first, when he'd left, she'd been furious with him. She'd told herself he'd regret it, that the shock of the pregnancy and the future before them had made him act without thought.

She'd done exactly as he'd said, returning to her own rooms, but she'd been angry. So angry.

And then, after four nights, she'd been lonely, and worried. After six nights, her worry had increased, because she still hadn't seen Malik. After ten days, she sucked up her pride and asked Awan where her husband was.

Awan had been surprised. The Sheikh was where he always was – in the palace.

Further digging revealed he'd only stayed away one night, before returning.

He wasn't sleeping in his room.

The first function she'd seen him at, he'd treated her like a stranger. Cordial, polite, touching her minimally, making only the most surface-level enquiries.

She'd been so furious, she'd planned to speak to him afterwards, but he'd had to take the helicopter straight over to another city, for a different function.

It had been the same at their next two engagements.

He looked at her and looked right through her.

"Just a small addition here," the woman said, running her finger down the side of the dress's panel. "And no one will notice a thing."

Sophia nodded, running a hand over her stomach. It was more rounded than she'd expected, so early on. Her sister Arabella had hardly showed in the first few months, but Sophia was already visibly pregnant – to anyone who looked closely – and it was still too early to want to make that announcement.

No doubt the gossip tabloids would speculate regardless – they always were – but Sophia wanted to wait to make a proper announcement.

She'd wait until she'd had the first scan, and perhaps by then, things with her and Malik would have resolved.

THE SCAN CAME AND WENT. He was there for it, standing beside her, his eyes fixed to the screen with a resolute sense of duty that made her want to shout at him to go away! This was their baby, if the most he could muster was a look of fierce and resentful obligation then she didn't want him there.

"And you are well?" He asked, when they were alone in her sitting room, the ultrasound equipment wheeled away, the doctor checking results in the kitchen.

She was. She'd been fine. At least, she'd told herself she had been. Two months since they'd argued, since she'd thought there was something between them from which she could make a real marriage. But his question, asked with a voice that was so carefully muted of any emotion, stirred something up inside of her.

"Oh, go to hell," she snapped, sitting up on the sofa, grabbing the towel to wipe the goo off her stomach. She felt the sting of tears at her eyes but refused to give into them.

She didn't see the way his features tightened, the way his expression shifted for a moment to one of pure anguish.

"The doctor says you have experienced some nausea."

She pushed up from the sofa, padding across the room and pouring a glass of ice water. "If you want to know how I'm feeling, ask me, not my doctor."

"I'm asking you now."

"But you already know the answer."

He compressed his lips and she felt like he was going to say something, but he didn't. He simply stared at her, dropping his gaze to her stomach, his eyes flashing with emotions she couldn't comprehend, and then he turned away, looking towards the windows.

Impatience zipped through her. She crossed the room, moving to stand in front of him, her eyes on his even when he looked past her.

"Look at me," she demanded, her expression grim.

For a moment, she thought he was going to refuse, but then, he dropped his gaze to hers, his face bearing a mask of absolute coldness.

It was galling, because she *knew* it wasn't how he felt. "I'm your wife," she said. "And this is our baby." She reached for his hand, and almost wished she hadn't when the spark of electricity that jolted through her at this physical contact almost knocked her sideways. Her breath grew rough. She lifted his hand anyway, hovering it over her stomach before curving his palm over the roundness there.

He closed his eyes and inhaled, and she stared at him, hoping for some kind of miracle. Hoping that when he looked at her once more it would be with a dawning realisation. An awakening. An acceptance of the truth of this – of the importance of reaching for what was right in front of them.

He looked at her, piercing her with his eyes, and then smiled. A perfunctory, banal, dismissive smile before he pulled his hand away and walked clear across the room.

Something inside of her burst.

"This is your child," she said softly but the words rang out with the weight of her pain. "And I am your wife. You don't get to walk out on us."

"I am right here," he demurred stiffly.

"You're nowhere," she said, shaking her head. "Did it occur to you that I miss you? That I need you in my life?"

A muscle jerked in his jaw and he shook his head. "You *need* my brother."

"Oh, for God's sake," she lifted a hand and pressed it to her brow. "Yes. I need Addan. You don't know how much I've wished I could talk to him, these last few months." She didn't flinch away from his gaze. "That's a part of how I feel. He's a part of me, a part of my heart. I loved him. He was my best friend. You have to accept that reality and still open yourself up to what's happening between us."

He shook his head. "I don't *have* to do anything."

"So you'd rather live your life like this, Malik?"

A muscle jerked in his jaw. "This life is… none of this is what I would rather."

She swallowed, the bitter truth of that impossible to avoid. Malik sought freedom, and always had. He'd run from this palace, from the rigours of royal life, preferring to be an individual rather than a prince. And now he was King, and married to a woman he couldn't ever admit to wanting.

"I will never say I didn't love him," she said quietly. "But I've realised something about you and me, Malik. I don't know when I first came to understand it, but these last months, not seeing you, not having you near me, how could I fail to realise what this pain is?" She pressed her fingers into her breastbone, her heart rabbiting hard beneath it. "I don't know when I fell in love with you, but somewhere in this marriage, I did. I love you, and I don't want to do this without you." She crossed the distance between them, lifting her hands to his chest, pressing them to his heart, hoping he would feel the urgency of hers even when he was standing there as a man of steel.

"Don't."

The word was like a whip. It cracked against her spine. She ignored the blinding pain. She had to fight for this, for him. She had to wake him up, to make him understand that what they were existed in a bubble that was completely separate to everything else.

"When I found out I was pregnant, I was over the moon. I was so happy. Not because it meant we'd achieved what we set out to, not because I thought it would somehow terminate what we'd been doing… I was thrilled because I couldn't think of anything I wanted more than to have a baby – to have a baby with *you*. No one else was in my mind; no one. This is about you and me, and the life we've created."

His head jerked back a little and his breathing was rough, his chest moving with the force of his exhalations. "Please stop."

It was the 'please' that got through to her. He was begging her. He was hurting, and she was rubbing his wounds raw. But god, she needed him to understand!

"I can't forget what you were to him. I can't forget that all of this is because he died – my brother. I am sorry, Sophia. It isn't fair to you, but I will never let this be more than a convenient marriage. You cannot speak of love to me –don't do it. It only makes me grieve for my brother, that your affections could be so easily transferred." His eyes were kind, even when his words were like bullets, exploding just under her skin.

Her pulse ratcheted up a notch and she shook her head, about to launch into another tirade, to explain that her affection hadn't been transferred, that it was different for each brother. There was no comparing how she felt. Addan had made her feel like she could rest, and Malik had pulled her back to life, he'd woken her up, every cell in her body, and she couldn't imagine ever not loving him.

But he was looking at her with cool dispassion once more. "The doctor wants to speak to you." He lifted his eyes over her shoulder, and she heard the door clicking shut.

"I'm sorry to interrupt, your highnesses."

Sophia had only a moment to rally her emotions, to pull them together, and then she turned to face him, her expression bearing a mask of calm that she was so far from feeling.

"The results look excellent, at this early stage," he said.

But something in his voice had Sophia's panic levels rising. "At this stage?"

He shook his head. "I wanted to double check the scans to be certain. Your highness," he addressed Malik and Sophia tried not to let it bother her. "There are two heartbeats."

Sophia's mind struggled to compute this. And then, she shook her head, and despite the heartbreak of a moment before, she smiled. "Do you mean we're having… twins?"

"Yes," the doctor drew his gaze back to Sophia's face. "And both are strong, showing good nutrient delivery. However, we will monitor you a little more closely than we would a single pregnancy."

"Of course," she smiled and nodded, and risked a glance at Malik. He was staring straight ahead, his face cast from stone.

She swallowed, and finished the conversation with the

doctor, scheduling her next appointment before seeing him to the door of the suite.

Alone again, she turned to face Malik, and she waited. Eventually, he dropped his eyes to hers and a shiver ran through her, for the coldness in his gaze.

"What's the matter?" She asked stiffly, shielding her heart out of habit now, protecting herself from the pain he seemed to inflict without making any such effort.

"The matter?" His own voice was flattened of any emotion. "Nothing, Sophia. You have done very well. Two children perfectly secures the bloodline – the purpose of our marriage has been met."

CHAPTER 14

THE NEXT NIGHT, SHE DREAMED that she'd followed him. That she'd thrown herself at him bodily and battered him with her small fists, that she'd screamed at him until he'd listened to her. That she'd pushed him to the floor and made love to him until he understood the truth of this.

But she didn't.

She watched him go with a heart that was turning cold, with a heart that was learning to accept the futility of trying to convince a man like Malik of anything. She watched him go with pure acceptance.

And doubts began to creep in. Not doubts as to her own feelings – she knew her heart and she understood it. But doubts as to his heart?

For love was not something that could be rejected so easily. She had offered him everything she was and he'd turned his back on her like it was nothing.

That was not love.

· · ·

SHE DISCOVERED, six weeks later, that he was having daily briefings about her. Usually, her chief of staff delivered them, but owing to illness, Awan had been dispatched to provide the update, and she'd mentioned it to Sophia almost in passing.

So he hadn't walked away from her completely.

Then again, she was carrying his royal heirs – he probably just wanted to know they were in good health.

AND THEY WERE. The same could not necessarily be said for Sophia.

"You must eat more," the doctor said, after her twenty-week ultrasound.

Worry immediately spread through her. "The babies?"

"They're fine," he murmured, lifting his gaze to Malik's face. "But you are not gaining enough weight. Growing twins is demanding on your body. If you don't look after yourself, you will suffer, your highness."

She felt Malik stiffen beside her. She didn't care. "I'm fine."

The doctor looked as though he wanted to argue, but Malik nodded, signalling that the matter was dealt with, and the doctor let himself out.

"Are you eating?"

She pushed up out of the sofa with more difficulty this time, her stomach was so much rounder. "Yes." She didn't meet his eyes. She couldn't. Pregnancy hormones were pulling her in a thousand different directions and she was afraid that if she looked into his eyes, she would burst into tears.

He was very still, she sensed his lack of movement and stayed where she was, head bent forward, eyes fixed on the carpet at her feet.

"Fine."

And he'd left.

BUT NOT FORGOTTEN, apparently. He returned at dinner, his expression grim. He watched her eat, and of course she barely ate anything, because her stomach was in knots having him sitting opposite her. "I'm not an animal in a zoo," she snapped, eventually, standing up and stalking towards her bathroom. "You don't get to come for feeding time and disappear again. You don't get to do that to me."

THE NEXT DAY, Awan sat with her while she ate. Awan chatted, telling Sophia all about her life, her childhood, her home, her sister's upcoming wedding, and Sophia nodded and smiled and answered back as she pushed food around her plate and ate what little she could, but inside, she fumed, because he was simply using Awan as a proxy.

She didn't want a proxy for her husband, and she didn't want a husband who saw her as a breeding machine.

But she did want two healthy babies. Only the doctor had been sure on that point – the twins were fine. It was only her own health that was suffering, and Sophia couldn't quite muster the energy to care.

It was too hot, and she was so fatigued, and growing all the more so every day.

WHEN SHE WAS six months pregnant, she did something she hadn't done in a very long time. She went into Addan's suite of rooms. She pushed the door open, and it was like stepping back in time. She latched it shut behind her, and simply stared. It was exactly as it had been, right before she'd gone to America to see Arabella. Right before he'd died.

Tears ran down her cheeks as she moved to his wardrobe and stepped inside, pulling one of his shirts from the drawer and lifting it to her face, bringing it with her to his bed. She lay down, just as she had so many nights, on her side, when they'd looked at each other and laughed and shared stories and she'd felt so happy, because it was all so simple.

He was her best friend.

She closed her eyes, hugging his shirt, feeling closer to him just by being here, and she fell asleep, completely oblivious to the explosive drama happening just a few feet away, within these very palace walls.

"You cannot simply lose the *Sharafaha*," he swore, Awan's face pale.

"She must have gone for a walk," Awan said, moving towards the windows. It was dark.

"Have I not asked you to watch her constantly?"

Panic grew in Awan's expression. "I didn't see her, she'd said she was tired, I thought she was going to lie down. I'm sure she said she was going to have a rest..."

Malik stalked to the bedroom and threw open the door. "Well, she is not here." He moved to the room next door – another bedroom, and inspected it. "Unless she's taken to sleeping under desks or pianos..."

"I will look for her," Awan said.

"You and the whole damned army," he swore, stalking to the door and alerting one of the guards. From between gritted teeth, panic shredding his insides: "Find my wife."

Twenty minutes later, he received the news. She'd been seen going into His Highness's quarters sometime that morning.

His stomach tightened at the very idea of her waiting for him in his rooms, of her sitting in that big chair, reading, or lying in his bed, fast asleep.

But the servant hadn't meant his room.

They'd meant Addan's.

His lips grim, he stalked the short distance from Sophia's apartment to Addan's. He didn't pause to brace himself at the door, and perhaps he should have, because the sight of Sophia fast asleep was enough to make his body lurch. But seeing her asleep in his brother's bed, holding an item of his brother's clothing to her breast, made him feel like his insides were being scraped out and replaced with acid. He stood there for several seconds and then, conscious that servants were right behind him, he turned, dismissing them.

He stared at her for several minutes, partly out of greed – he had not had this luxury in many long months. And partly from a disturbed place of self-punishment.

No matter what she said, no matter what promises she made, nothing changed this. Nothing changed the love she felt for Addan, nor he for her.

That was what was real here. He couldn't blame her for trying to make the best out of their marriage, for desperately attempting to create some kind of bond between them, beyond the physical. But it was a futile, unnecessary exercise.

He could never love this woman.

He could never love the woman who should have been married to his brother.

It was bad enough that Addan had been robbed of his life and his crown, but to also lose this woman's heart?

Malik had to protect at least that.

Addan deserved no less.

He stepped out of the room, leaving the door open. He spoke to a guard as he left. "Check on her regularly and notify me when she wakes."

. . .

A MONTH PASSED and when he next had to see Sophia, he braced for it. He recalled that image of her curled up in Addan's bed, and he held it tight in his chest and mind.

She was Addan's.

He was prepared to see her, his heart like ice, but when she walked towards the car, Awan on one side and a servant he didn't recognise on the other, everything inside of him shattered, every certainty he'd felt that he was doing the right thing detonated like a bomb.

They were due at the opening of a children's hospital, but there was no way he could let go anywhere.

He stepped away from the car.

"Send our apologies," he said to Awan, putting a hand in the small of Sophia's back and almost swearing when he felt the ridges of her spine.

"What are you doing?" She demanded, her expression one of hauteur. His chest cracked.

"You are not leaving the house like this."

"Like what?" She looked down at the robes she wore – a stunning blue with gems around the collar.

"Come inside." He gently propelled her back into the palace, his heart pounding so hard and fast he could hear his blood rushing. "Please."

Please. God, please, he prayed mentally, watching her warily, waiting for her. But she shook her head. "We're expected at the hospital. This is important. I've been on the fundraising committee for years. I'm not missing it."

He ground his teeth together, staring at her, hating himself in that moment for what he'd done to this beautiful creature. Hating himself and life desperately.

"You are too slender," he said, the words croaking from him.

Her eyes showed defiance when they lifted to his. "I'm fine. And I'm going to this event; I'm a patron, for God's sake. Are you going to come with me?"

He swore under his breath and turned around, staring at the car, his expression grim. "For thirty minutes," he said, finally. "And then home."

She lifted her eyes to his, and there was such desolate loss there, such chasming emptiness that his stomach dropped to his feet. "Home?" Her laugh was brittle. "Where the hell is home?"

HE WATCHED HIS CLOCK. Thirty minutes hadn't been a joke, nor a number he'd pulled from thin air. He watched his wife speak to the other board members, and the medical chiefs of departments, and while he felt admiration for her abilities, he also felt alarm. Alarm that she'd deteriorated so much in a month. Alarm that skin which had once glowed translucent like crushed pearls was now so thin and fine he could see grey beneath her eyes despite the skilled application of makeup. Her hair was darker, her lips thinner, and her whole body was so slim he had no idea how she was managing to stay upright with the huge baby bump out front.

Twenty nine minutes after arriving, he called an end to it, practically frog marching her back to the limousine.

His worry grew as they drove back to the palace in complete silence. She made no efforts to talk to him, she didn't attempt a conversation. She simply stared out of her window, and he stared at her, cataloguing the changes and knowing each and every one was his fault.

His responsibility.

Sophia had come to this kingdom as a child. A beautiful, free-spirited child. She was not of this land, of these people, but she had come to exemplify the Abu Fayan spirit. She was the magic of this place. She had been wild and free and beautiful and bold, and bit by bit he had strangled that from her.

He must have made some kind of audible noise of disgust because she jerked her face to his suddenly. Their eyes met and his heart turned over in his chest because when she looked at him, he saw none of the spark in her eyes that was so uniquely Sophia.

He saw nothing, and felt everything.

WHEN THE CAR pulled up at the palace, he stepped out and opened her door before a servant could, reaching for her wordlessly. She stared at him like he'd taken leave of all of his senses, and perhaps he had.

She didn't move and so, with frustration, he bent down and scooped her up, cradling her against his chest, carrying her through the palace, his face bearing a mask of utter resignation.

He took her to his apartment, to the suite of rooms he'd cajoled her to move into before asking her to vacate once more. His gut churned at the way he'd behaved that day.

"I don't want to be here," she said, pushing from his chest as soon as they walked in. He carried her to the sofa and settled her down before standing and staring at her as though she were a puzzle he had to fathom.

"You must stay with me now."

"No." She jack-knifed out of the seat, her eyes glaring at his and the spark was back, but it was a spark of angry defiance. "Never again."

His jaw clenched tight.

"You aren't well."

"I'm fine. I'm seeing the doctor every week."

He knew that to be the case. He'd been getting the

reports, and yet nothing had been said of Sophia's health – only the babies'.

"I feel like you are about to snap in two. You cannot be eating."

Her eyes showed pure disdain. "I'm doing the best I can, Malik."

"You are doing too much, then. You must scale back on your duties and focus only on this."

"This is my duty," she pointed out scathingly, swallowing, and he recalled saying that to her when he'd left her, after the first ultrasound appointment. "And it's almost discharged. Your heirs are almost here. You have nothing to worry about."

"I don't care about that, Sophia. I care about you. I care about your health. And it's so obviously failing…"

"I'm fine," she wiped her palms on her stomach and turned away from him. "The twins are taking up too much room. They're pressing on my stomach. I can't eat, even if I… even if I wanted to feast, I couldn't. Awan makes me juices and smoothies. I have more success with them. I'm doing my best."

His heart pulled, because he believed her. He had to believe her. This wasn't some kind of self-sabotage. She wasn't so miserable that she was hunger-striking her way out of this marriage.

Only she *was* miserable. He knew that to be the case. He saw the light inside of her had been extinguished and his body flooded with anger. Self-directed anger.

"I want you to stay here. I want to help you until this is over and you are back to normal."

Her laugh was hollow. "No."

"Why not? I am your husband."

"My husband?" She shook her head angrily. "You are no such thing." She moved towards the door, pulling it inwards.

"Out there, we can pretend, but when it's just us, let's call a spade a spade. You're my sperm donor, and I'm your womb, and very soon you'll have the only thing you care about. So just leave me alone to do this."

HER WORDS PRESSED down on him like an enormous weight. He heard them in his dreams – nightmares, more like – and he felt them in his mouth like acid when he was awake.

But why wouldn't she feel that way? At every point, he'd made it obvious he wanted her for one reason only.

The line of succession.

Babies.

The future of the palace.

This wasn't about them. It wasn't about the way his heart soared when he thought of the children she was growing. This was… it was such a mess.

He told himself he couldn't upset her again, not while she was pregnant. Once the babies were born, he would talk to her. He would find a way to bring her spark back, to make her smile. Not like Addan had, but like he – Malik – could. He would find a way to bring lightness to the dark.

"IT IS TOO hot to walk, your highness, and you are eight and a half months pregnant."

Sophia flicked her gaze to Awan's. "Thank you, I'm very aware of that." She took a sip of her water and grabbed her hat. "I'm only going to get some rosemary. I won't be long."

"Then I'll come with you—,"

Sophia reached out and put a reassuring hand on Awan's forearm. "I want to be alone. Please."

She didn't tell Awan why. No one else seemed to remember that today was Addan's birthday, but she did.

She'd felt the tug of his memories since she'd woken and now, with dusk approaching, she could bear it no longer. She had to be alone. To think of him, to sit quietly and feel his absence. To honour his memory.

The kitchen garden had the best collection of rosemary, but there were servants there – always tending to it, collecting its spoils for the palace kitchens. And so she chose the pomegranate grove, where wild rosemary could be found in clumps.

And on autopilot, she made her way to the single bush in the corner, where she and Addan had been playing that one hot day – much like this one – so many years earlier. She'd pricked her finger and he'd wound a bandage to stop it from bleeding. And eight year old Sophia, who had yet to learn anything of loss and life's cruelties, had smiled into a pair of kind eyes, and they'd smiled back, and she'd felt like she'd come home.

Was she living out a foolish fantasy now? Had she clung so hard to Addan because he'd crystallised a perfect moment in a life that was about to be turned on its head? When her father had died, she'd lost two parents –her mother had given up any pretence of behaving in a maternal fashion, and her sister had been sent away, to live with Spanish Godparents.

Sophia had needed to feel at home somewhere, and Bashira had made her so welcome. Addan had made her so welcome.

And Malik had made her feel alive – hating him had set her soul on fire when it had been almost dead. She ran her finger over the pomegranate bush, avoiding the spikes, and her stomach twinged. She sobbed. Grief.

It overtook her.

"Happy birthday, my friend," she said, dipping her head forward, so that her tears fell on the scorched earth beneath.

. . .

SHE STAYED A LONG TIME, until the sun had set and darkness had wrapped its way around the palace. She picked a small handful of rosemary – for remembrance – on her way back inside.

Her stomach twinged once more.

Before she reached the steps, there was a pain low in her abdomen and then water was gushing down her legs.

"Awan!" She called at the top of her lungs, turning around. For once, there were no guards. "Awan!" She grabbed the railing and moved up one step, but there was another pain. She called for her servant once more, and then felt darkness descending – she sat down before she fell.

"HER HIGHNESS IS IN LABOUR," the message came to Malik while he was in the middle of a dinner with several of his high-ranked ministers. His mind though had been on Sophia, as it almost always was. He scraped his chair back, leaving the room without another word.

"Where is she?"

"En route to the hospital already," his servant said.

"What happened?"

The servant shook his head. "I am not certain, sir."

"How is she?"

The servant shook his head. "I cannot say."

Malik began to run, his pulse like fire in his blood. He couldn't get to her fast enough.

"WHERE IS SHE?"

The doctor was shouting instructions and Malik's blood pounded harder. "Doctor?"

"You cannot go to her," he said, not looking up from the charts he was reading.

"Where is my wife?"

The doctor spoke low and fast to the assembled team and then nodded, so they scattered like leaves in the breeze, before turning to the Sheikh. "She's in the operating theatre."

"Why?"

"There were complications." The doctor's expression was grim.

"Doctor, I command you to tell me whatever it is you're holding back. I want to know everything."

THE TWINS WERE FINE. Sophia fought hard for them, even when her body was turning against her. They emerged robust and bright red, their cries loud and confident. Malik heard them from outside the Operating theatre and emotions swarmed inside of him.

He'd been told he couldn't enter, that the room was sterile and with twins there were too many specialists on call – that it would be too crowded for another.

And a man who was used to being universally obeyed found himself deferring to the doctor even when every cell in his body was demanding he burst into the room and see for himself. See his children. See his wife.

His wife.

God. Please let her be okay now the twins had been born.

He waited, his breath partly held, his body frozen.

Then, there was a noise. A shout, and an alarm sounded. Medical teams came running. Doctors and nurses from all directions, moving in one direction.

All into Sophia's room.

He couldn't wait any longer.

He pushed inside in time to see a machine hooked up to

Sophia's chest, and everyone clearing while the instrument was read, then moving back with urgency. Her stomach had been cut – the babies had been born via caesarean. She was so pale. Like the sands of the desert.

Her eyes were shut. He couldn't help it. He moved to her, closer, his throat thick as he couldn't tear his eyes away. He looked down at her, her beautiful face so restful now, like she was asleep. And he made a guttural noise from deep within him. Her eyes lifted, slowly, with difficulty.

He felt the moment she recognised him and his chest exploded.

"They're here," she spoke without smiling. "Your babies."

"Our babies." He reached for her hand, squeezing it. She didn't say anything. Not for a long time, and the medical staff worked frantically, pressing against her chest, doing everything they could to mend her body.

"Love them, Malik," she said, the words obviously costing her a great effort. "Love them even when you want to push them away," she paused, closing her eyes, and he realised she was crying, tears rolling down the side of her face. "With all that you are, please love them for me."

Sophia had always been a fighter but finally, all the fight had left her.

CHAPTER 15

"NO." HE SAID THE WORD to no one and everyone. He looked around the room at the people who were working frantically on his wife. She'd fallen asleep. She'd left him.

She was gone.

But he couldn't let her be.

He stared at her and took a step backwards, his body disconnected from his mind.

"You will make her well," he roared, and he stared at her, but he had no hope. Nor any reason to hope. Why would life be so good to return her to him?

Why would fate reward him with her?

He'd been given the gift of this woman and he'd rejected it at every turn.

He hadn't deserved her.

He held himself perfectly still as they worked, watching every man and woman, waiting, his body on tenterhooks. He could not look at his children, despite what she'd asked of him. He didn't even know if they were boys or girls.

He stared at Sophia, her pale face growing more pale by the second, and he felt the world was swallowing him whole.

He knelt down beside her and did the only thing he could: he prayed.

"Don't you leave me, Sophia." He dropped his head forward, to hers. "Don't you think of going anywhere."

FOUR DAYS LATER, he hadn't left her side. She remained in a coma, but he spoke to her as though she were awake. He brought their children to her, their babies, two beautiful girls, and he described them in every detail to her.

On the fifth day, he began to read. He read Plato, just as his mother had read to him and Addan as children. He read Plato because he knew she loved it, and because he loved it, and because she had been right about how much they had in common.

He read Plato because it was something she'd shared with Addan and just maybe memories of his brother would stir into her mind, and bring her to life. And he wouldn't even mind – he wouldn't feel envy, not if it meant Sophia came back to him.

He read Plato and he refused to contemplate a world in which she didn't wake up.

ON THE SEVENTH day of her coma, he could no longer bear the grim expressions of the nurses. He asked for only one doctor – the one who didn't look at him as though he were the only fool in the room who didn't understand what was happening – to attend to her.

And he read Plato again, the words like an incantation, a spell, a way to magic her back to him. And sometimes, he fantasised about what that would look like. If only there was a way he could wipe away the last eight months, and take them back to the desert. To the way she'd fought so hard for their marriage, the way she'd counselled him and delighted in the people of the desert.

Even then he'd fought her. He'd pushed her away, when he'd wanted to pull her into his arms and make her his in every possible way.

His chest felt like it was going to crush and finally, he gave into the sense of brokenness that had been dogging him since then. Since he'd discovered she was pregnant and thrown the first stone that would eventually break the glass of their marriage.

He dropped his head forward, and a sob wracked from his body, the first time he'd cried since his mother had died. This was a grief unlike any other, though. There was so much guilt in it, and so much anger, so much self-recrimination and pain, because this was all his fault. His foolish, foolish fault.

"You cannot go," he said, and lifted his lips to her forehead, pressing a kiss there, feeling her warmth that was all a courtesy of the machines she was hooked up to. "You cannot leave me. You cannot leave them. Sophia, don't go."

SOPHIA HAD ALWAYS BEEN A FIGHTER, and even with her body in a coma she heard his words, they called to her, and later that same day something flickered to life, shifting in her body.

She blinked her eyes open and it was like waking from the strangest, most disconcerting dream. Everything within her body felt different. She was sore and heavy.

And she was alone.

Her eyes flew wider. Her head screamed in complaint. She pushed up, looking around. Nothing made sense. But the twins – she threw the blanket off and stared at her stomach. It wasn't flat, but it was closer to it, and when she pressed a hand to her stomach, she knew there was no one there.

"Oh my God," it made no sense. She looked around the room again and her eyes landed on Malik in a black armchair, his eyes shut. Her heart twisted. She skated her eyes past him, and now she saw the hospital equipment and realised she was hooked up to a thousand machines. She collapsed back against the pillows, and perhaps this motion roused Malik because he was by her side instantly.

Staring at her as though he couldn't believe it really was her, as though she were some kind of demon or ghost, staring at her as though she were a miracle.

"Where—," her voice came out as a very dry whisper. She swallowed; it was an agony.

He reached for a plastic cup on her bedside and held it to her lips. Her eyes met his when she drank, but she couldn't hold his gaze. It hurt too much. Everything hurt.

"Twins," she croaked, afterwards.

He nodded. "They're fine. Two girls." He reached across her again and pressed a button. His expression was so grim, she was certain he was lying to her.

"Tell me, Malik. Tell me what's happened." It hurt to speak.

He shook his head, pressing a hand to hers, so her pulse throbbed in her body, distributing her blood. "You had complications. HELLP syndrome, and an irregularity in your heart. You passed out, and the doctor put you into a coma while your body healed…"

Blurs came back to her. Memories of being wheeled into an operating theatre, patchy and as if through a very long period of time. She shook her head. It was like a dream. She couldn't speak those words. Her throat was raw. "The babies," she said instead.

If she didn't know Malik as well as she did, she'd have said he was surfing some strong emotional currents of his own. His expression was carefully guarded, but his eyes showed feelings that were overwhelming in their intensity. "I promise you, *Sharafaha*, they are fine." And perhaps because he'd realised she couldn't speak easily, he continued, "Two beautiful girls, one so like you it takes my breath away, and the other like Addan." He squeezed her hand, and right as the door pushed open, he said, "They were born on his birthday, you know."

More memories. The pomegranates and rosemary. Her tiredness. Exhaustion. Grief.

She swallowed, turning towards the doctor.

"Your highness," he nodded, his smile reassuring. "You're awake." He spent a few minutes checking her vitals, and then turned to Malik. "Her progress is excellent. We'll keep her here for a few more days, to monitor for any complications, and then her highness will be discharged. However, she'll need monitoring at the palace, too –,"

"You can suggest someone?"

"I'm happy to attend," the doctor nodded brusquely. "And to arrange nursing staff."

Sophia cleared her throat. It still hurt. "I want to see them."

Malik nodded. "Of course." He looked to the doctor. "You'll arrange for our daughters to be brought?"

"At once." The doctor turned to Sophia once more, smiling. "I am glad to see you awake."

Sophia managed a weak smile of her own, and once alone with Malik again, she felt the butterflies ramming her insides. The enormity of what was about to happen settled about her shoulders.

But it was more than just seeing her twins. It was everything that came next. She was a mother. They were parents. A family.

A hollow feeling settled inside of her, because they were nothing of the sort and never would be. Children didn't change a thing – not in terms of how Malik felt for her. Grief – the same grief that had gnawed at her throughout her pregnancy – clouded her mind.

She blinked, focussing on a bright white light switch across the room.

"I thought you would never wake up," he said, moving to the side of the bed, his arms crossed as he looked at her with an intensity that she felt, even when not lifting her eyes to his.

"How long?"

"A week." The word was tortured. "Seven days, seven nights – it might as well have been a lifetime."

She swallowed. There was so much she wanted to say, but her throat wasn't up to it.

"Drink."

He nodded, bringing the cup back to her lips. She sipped it, and it helped, immensely. When the doctor returned, he held some tablets in his hand. "Painkillers." He watched as she swallowed them and, seconds later, the twins were wheeled in, each in their own little crib. She held her breath then. A nurse propped her up with pillows, and put more on either side, before bringing one of the children to her. She stared at her daughter and her heart exploded.

She felt – everything. Nothing mattered beyond this perfection.

The second twin was brought and placed into the other arm, so Sophia had both her children in her lap. She stared at them for a long time, noting every detail, silently communicating with them. They had lived inside of her and she had given them life.

Gratitude exploded within Sophia – gratitude that she was here, with them, that the pregnancy complications hadn't robbed her of this. She dropped her head forward, placing a kiss on each forehead. Her arms hurt and her head grew heavy but she refused to say as much.

Malik noticed though. He leaned closer, so only she could hear. "You are tired. We will put the twins here, in their cribs, so you can watch them as you fall asleep."

Her heart squeezed, because it was exactly what she needed. She had already missed too much of their little lives – she didn't want to miss another breath.

She woke several hours later, much stronger and well-feeling, and immediately looked for her children. One slept in the crib, the other was on Malik's lap, a bottle in his competent, large hands. The sight of her husband feeding their daughter tied her up in knots. She swallowed for a different reason now – her throat was no longer lined with razor blades but filling with the taste of salty tears.

Sensing her movement, Malik lifted his head, pinning her with his gaze. Their eyes locked, neither able to pull away, and grief threatened to return to Sophia despite the perfection of the two people they'd created.

"This one is always hungry," he said with a smile, a slow smile that set fire to her soul. "She has my brother's eyes and my appetite."

The sob surprised Sophia. She lifted her hands to her eyes, pushing against them, turning her face away at the same time. Malik stood, she heard him, even when she wasn't looking at him. He came to her bed and perched on its edge, still holding their daughter in his hands.

"I had no idea if you would come back to me, Sophia," he said, the words gravelled. "I have spent this week imagining what I would say to you if this happened, and now that you're before me, awake, I find the words won't come out."

She kept her face averted.

"I imagined apologising to you, but not being able to find the right way – what could I say that would sufficient for what I had done?"

Her throat hurt again. She squeezed her eyes shut; hot tears burned against her eyelids.

"Every time I thought I knew what I would say to you, I closed my eyes and remembered your pain, remembered the generosity of your heart that had you trying so hard to make me see… to make me understand… and the way I failed you, because I refused to even listen."

She bit back another sob, her heart was trembling. "You were honest with me," she said, after a moment, when she could trust her voice to speak.

"I do not think I was even honest with myself, *Sharafaha.*"

He lifted a hand, brushing her hair behind her ear.

"All I cared about was pushing you away. We had to sleep together, for the sake of an heir, to validate this marriage, but that was all. I was determined. And I clung to that even when you begged me to open my eyes and see the truth."

"Malik," she bit down on her lip, her eyes finally lifting to his. She felt like she was being drowned. "You made me open *my* eyes, to see *your* truth, and I get it. I understand. You will never be able to separate guilt towards Addan from our marriage, and I'm not going to try to make you. We have the twins, we have your heirs. It is enough."

He was quiet for a moment. "And is this enough for you?"

Her eyes dropped to the baby in his arms, and a small smile shifted on her pale face. "These children will become my world. This *will* be enough."

He made a guttural, groaning noise and shook his head. "Not for me, and not I think for you, either. Sophia, you came to Abu Faya and nothing has ever been the same since. From the first moment I saw you and Addan together, I hated you. I told myself it was your Americanness, then that I was jealous – Addan had been my closest friend until you, and then, everything was 'Sophia this', 'Sophia that'."

"I didn't mean to displace you," she said, reluctantly, because there was nothing good that could come from discussing the past.

He leaned closer to her, and she held her breath, her heart telling her to be strong, to fight this, to fight the temptation to sink into him.

"You took my breath away, from the first moment I saw you. But it was at your seventeenth birthday when I realised what I felt wasn't jealousy of you, for your friendship with Addan."

Her eyes closed as she remembered that night – his palpable anger. "I was so jealous of Addan. He announced your betrothal and I wanted to lift you up and take you away, to hide you all for me. I wanted you all for myself, Sophia."

She shook her head – it wasn't true. There was no way that made sense. "You hated me."

"Yes. I hated you. I hated you because of how you made me feel. Addan and I had been so close, but knowing you would marry him, I began to hate him, too. To feel such envy that it sickened me. He was my brother and I found myself wishing our place in the order of succession had been reversed. I found myself wishing my father had thought you would be a suitable bride for me. When Addan died…"

"Don't." She shook her head. "You didn't will that."

"Didn't I?" He glared at her and she felt the cold despair in his heart. "I didn't care for his throne or rule, but I wanted you in a way that appalled me. I told myself the only way to atone for how I had envied him and coveted you was to ensure our relationship was never more than sex. He had held your heart, and taking that from him was too low. It was too much to hope you might love me, as you had him. I had to content myself with your body."

His words were striking against her sides. She heard them but wanted to roll them up and throw them back at him. She wanted... she felt stronger now, fight filling her.

"I told you again and again that what I had with Addan was different."

"Yes. And I was so glad for that. Glad that you were so much happier with him. Glad that he was the man you had chosen to marry. Remembering that I was your consolation husband almost stopped me from wanting more from you."

"I gave you more," she said with impatient disbelief. "I gave you everything."

"Yes," he admitted, his nod a jerk of his head. Their daughter had drunk all of her bottle. He lifted her over his shoulder, burping her gently, and then passed the little one to Sophia. She cradled their daughter, her heart twisting inside her chest. "You gave me everything, and it only made me more determined. The more you tried to convince me we could be friends, the more I insisted we wouldn't be. When you told me you loved me, I wanted to die, Sophia, for how much I craved those words. He was my brother." The last sentence was anguished. "And you were his fiancé. He loved you, so much. He loved you and to hear you say you love me... I was so angry."

"I remember." She swallowed.

"But I wasn't angry with you. I was furious with this life – with fate – with the fact you'd been chosen for him, and acquiesced so readily to those wishes. I was furious that you and I hadn't simply met, two people, unencumbered by any of this. I was so angry that what my heart wanted felt impossible to attain."

She dropped her head forward, her eyes filling with tears once more.

"I told you, this is different. You cannot compare what Addan and I were to one another to what you and I... to what we... had." She finished softly, because it all felt so different. She didn't doubt her own heart – love was not so fickle. Having fallen for Malik, she knew she would always love him like this. But the connection she'd imagined had been eroded by his months of coldness and rejection, so that even now, hearing his explanation, her feelings remained shielded deep within her.

"At seventeen, I told myself things would change. You were still so young. You had no concept of what you'd agreed to – maybe you would change your mind, or your mother would refuse to let you go ahead with this. I went away, yet every time I came back, you were happier and more adored, and I realised you would never be mine. Wanting you and seeing you with him was torture. I taught myself to hate you, to hate your wedding, to disapprove of it in every way, to stop myself from acting on these feelings."

His eyes bore into hers. "You do not know how often I dreamed of that – you beneath me, calling my name. I hated my own brother, Sophia, because of how much I wanted you." He stood up then, pacing away from her, his back ramrod straight.

"When he died, and your betrothal passed to me, I wanted to push you away because I have no doubt I willed this."

"Stop it," she snapped then, and the daughter in her lap startled. She lowered her voice with great effort. "What happened to Addan was a terrible accident."

He whirled around. "And if he'd lived, you would have married him. And I would have spent my lifetime wanting my brother's wife. Do you not see how there was gladness inside of me?"

She shook her head angrily and then, sympathy exploded. "You say you hated your brother, but I see the actions of a man who sacrificed what he wanted, again and again, out of respect for his brother."

A muscle jerked in Malik's jaw.

"I see a man who chose to respect his brother's wishes even when it brought him pain. You didn't fail Addan, Malik."

"I could not be in the same room as the two of you."

"He never suspected why," she promised. "He went to his grave with no idea you felt any of this. But I know, because he was my best friend and we talked about anything and everything," she saw her husband stiffen and hated paining him. "That he adored you and admired you in every way."

His eyes were haunted. "It … means so much to me." His eyes swept shut for a moment. "I could not bear him to have known how I longed for you…"

"Believe me, he didn't," she promised. "He was saddened that we didn't get on. He had no idea there was anything behind that."

"I couldn't be with you, Sophia. I couldn't be in the same room as you without wanting to kiss you, to touch you, to make you laugh."

"Damn you." The curse growled from deep within her chest. She straightened, so she could gently place their daughter in her crib, and then she stood, gingerly, the scar from her surgery still tender. She walked to him with care, and he watched her. "Damn you for not saying anything." She lifted her hands then, cupping his cheeks. "And for not telling me any of this sooner. I have been in agony; you have made me miserable. And now? You're telling me this is why you pushed me away?"

He groaned, cupping her cheeks. "He was my brother and I … have taken so much from him. It is not 'nothing.'"

"No, but it is separate from us." She spoke quietly, as though it were simple.

"You were so close to marrying him…"

"You don't know that. Neither of us knows that. Addan and I, as close as we were, there was no chemistry between us. We hadn't really even kissed, Malik." Her teeth dug into her lower lip, as she tried to put words to how she'd felt. "When my dad died, I lost my whole family. Everything changed. And your dad and Addan replaced them, they made me feel whole again. I had a new family, who adored me, and welcomed me."

"Except for me."

"Yes, except for you," she said with a quiet nod. "And I was too young to look at the damage I was doing and to care. I was just a child, Malik."

"I know that." He cleared his throat. "You told me, that at Addan's birthday, his last birthday, you realised you desired me."

Her eyes lifted to his, the memory so clear in her mind. "I had never felt anything like it. Lust tore me apart. I wanted you. *You*, Malik. Even then."

He moved closer, his face so near hers. "And it just made me furious, because I thought about you that night. You have no idea how close I came to stealing you away, to taking you into the desert, away from all of this, to telling you how I felt and hoping against hope you might feel the same."

"But you didn't."

"No. You gave me no reason to hope. You were so cold to me." He padded his thumb over her cheek. "So when Addan died, it was easy to see your grief, to know what you had lost. We were to marry, and your body would be mine. I had no business wanting any other part of you. Even when it was offered."

"But it was *offered*," she said, taking a step backwards,

even when all she wanted was to stay right there, close to him, feeling his heat and warmth. "I chose you."

"You chose nothing." His eyes swept shut. "You were chosen for Addan and he died, leaving you to me..."

"Do you think you are the only one who had been fighting this?" She shook her head gently, her expression showing anguish. "Addan was so safe, Malik. He adored me and I him, and I knew we would spend the rest of our lives in a very relaxed, respectful friendship. I had lost so much – my father's death changed me. I didn't want the highs and lows of a passionate affair. I just wanted calm, easy content- ment. Addan and I were perfectly suited in that regard. But you were like a sinkhole. If you were in the room, you were all I could think of, all I could look towards. Instinctively I fought this, and you, but I don't think I could have fought it forever. I think, after Addan's birthday, something would have changed. I don't think two people can be so right for one another as you and I are and not find their way eventually."

He made a guttural noise, rushing his hands through his hair, dislodging it from the messy bun. "You say that and yet, look what it took? You almost died. I have had to look down the barrel at life without you to realise that no guilt for Addan could prevent me from being honest with you."

He groaned, moving towards her. "If you had died and never known how sorry I was, how wrong I have been, Sophia, it would have killed me. I fell in love with you so long ago, and I had to fight it. I had to fight wanting you, needing you, craving you. And it became a habit, a habit that didn't die with my brother. I don't want to fight you anymore."

Her sob was completely involuntary. She swallowed it as best as she could.

He wrapped an arm around her back, pulling her towards

him gently, mindful of her scars – physical and emotional – mindful that all would take time to heal.

"I stared at you and I read Plato to you, and I kept hearing a quote from it, chasing itself around and around my mind." He dropped his head, kissing her forehead because he could no longer resist. *"I am the wisest man alive –"*

"For I know one thing," she interrupted. *"And that is that I know nothing."*

He nodded jerkily. "I thought I had all the answers. I thought I could keep you boxed away in one place, that I could give you one aspect of myself and take one aspect of yours, and that it would be like an addict having a very small fix. I thought it would in some way mitigate my betrayal of Addan, if I didn't overwrite everything he'd meant to you, if I didn't demand your heart as well as your body."

He dropped his head lower, brushing his lips over hers, and her heart squeezed.

"I thought I had all the answers, but I knew nothing. You were never going to be kept in one small box of my life, and nor should you have been. My father was right to select you as Sheikha – you are the most spectacular woman I have ever known. You have spread into my life, into all parts of my soul. I fell in love with you so long ago, Sophia, but I have fallen in love with you again and again, every day of our marriage." He wrapped her tighter, close to his body.

"I know I cannot say anything here that will take away the damage I have caused. I know it will take time for you to forgive me, to let me back in. But I want, more than anything, to earn my place at your side, Sophia Bin Hazari."

It was too much. His anguish was too much. "Stop it."

He was very still for a moment and then he dropped his hands to his side.

"Addan was my best friend. Not for anything on this earth would I have risked hurting him. Can you not see how much more it makes me love you, to know you were willing to walk away from me even when it hurt you, hurt me, all for Addan? You loved him, and you cared for him and respected him. There is no guilt here for you to bear. If our marriage is a resurrection from the ashes of his death, I can't feel bad about that. Until the day he died, we were faithful to him, to his wishes."

Malik swallowed roughly, she felt the movement.

"You were faithful to Addan and knowing now what that cost you, it makes me care for you even more. There is only goodness in what you did."

He groaned. "You are rewriting my actions…"

"No. I'm holding a mirror up and showing you that you can be proud of your conduct with Addan. You sacrificed for him. You were a good brother."

"And a terrible husband."

She lowered her eyes, her heart strangely light, her chest tingling. "There's room for improvement," she conceded, after a beat.

"Will you let me improve?"

She frowned, looking to him.

"I have had seven days to think about this, Sophia, to think about how I can fix this. And I have to say this to you. You have any option at your disposal that you would wish. Stay here in Abu Faya as my Sheikh, but never see me again, if that is your wish. Stay here in Abu Faya and divorce me, and I will ensure you never worry about anything, all your life. Go back to America; I will understand all these things. These are the options I should have presented you, that night he died, but I didn't. I couldn't. I wasn't strong enough then to let you go."

"And you are now?"

"Keeping you here and watching a part of you die because you are so miserable is not something I can do a second time." His expression was ash. "Seeing you fade from me, these last few months, knowing myself impotent to fix it, God, Sophia, I cannot do that again. Choose what will make you happy and let me give that to you. Your happiness is all I care for now."

So much grief flew from her and there was only relief in its place. "You want to make me happy?"

"With all my heart. I must."

She nodded. "Fine. Then let me tell you what I want."

And he held his breath, waiting, his expression one of pure wariness.

"Be my husband." Her eyes bore into his. "Be my husband in every way. Talk to me, laugh with me, share your life with me. Your worries, your frustrations, your triumphs. Let me take my place at your side, as your Sheikha and as your wife. Your partner in all things. Be the parent to our children that I know you are."

He didn't speak. He only stared at her.

"Take me to the desert, often. Take me to those magical people, to be a part of their life and culture. Love me, Malik, without guilt, without fear. Love me completely." She lifted up onto the tips of her toes, pressing a kiss against his lips. He groaned and deepened it, holding her right where she was, his tongue duelling with hers, the force of his relief evident in every cell of his body.

"I promise you, Sophia, all of this, and all of me."

"And I promise you I will be happy from now on," she said, smiling, because she knew, without even a hint of doubt, that it was absolutely true. She had everything she needed, and always would, for evermore.

THE END

212 | CLARE CONNELLY

I hope you loved Sophia and Malik's story! This is the fifth
book in the bestselling Evermore series.

I would be so grateful if you'd take a moment to leave a quick
star rating or review now that you're finished THE
SHEIKH'S INHERITED BRIDE.

Read on for an exclusive excerpt from Book Two of THE MONTEBELLOS, JUST THIS ONE SUMMER, which will be available in October 2019.

You can pre-order the E-book for the special price of 99c until its release date.

Happy reading, and don't forget to leave a review if you have a moment.

EXCERPT - JUST THIS ONE SUMMER

AVAILABLE OCTOBER 2019 - PREORDER NOW!

PROLOGUE

S HE DIDN'T PACK MUCH. One bag, just enough to throw over the shoulder and carry with ease. Enough to keep her going until she found her feet. Enough to help her get away – to get away quickly. She didn't know where she was going, but she knew she had to leave. Immediately. Madeleine left without looking back, because looking back hurt too much.

If she looked back long enough, she'd see Michael as he'd been when they first met. Charming, handsome, kind, everything she'd ever thought she'd wanted.

But new memories had overwritten those quickly enough. The smell of alcohol on his breath. The way his voice went quiet and soft when he was angry; somehow, that was so much more frightening than when he yelled. The certainty his temper was always worse when he'd bet big and lost bigger. And finally, the feeling of his hand around her throat, the way breath had burned in her lungs, the way her eyes had ached, darkness encroaching until she'd remembered she had legs and had lifted one, kneeing him in the groin. It wasn't hard but it was enough.

She'd never fought back before. Then again, he'd never made it so imperative that she did.

Looking over her shoulder was an impulse. She did it now, twisting her head so her blonde ponytail flicked in the breeze, making sure no one saw her get on the bus. Her heart was slamming against her ribs, her breathing was still rushed. As the bus whistled out of Putney, it occurred to Madeleine that she had no idea where she was going.

She knew though that she would no longer be Madeleine Gray. She'd be Maddie. Someone different to this. Someone stronger. Someone who'd never be fooled again. Someone who was independent. Solitary. Safe.

She watched from the window as the bus rounded the corner. Shops she knew so well – the Tesco express, the bank, the post office, a Wagamamas, all so familiar to her, but all relegated to the back of her mind, to the past.

Another bus and an overground and she'd arrived at Heathrow, and by then, Maddie had a plan.

It didn't come to her perfectly formed. But when she closed her eyes and imagined peace and tranquillity, she saw a place with a musical name, a place she'd found herself wondering about for no reason in particular, a place she was eager now to go to. It didn't make sense, it was as though her soul was being called on in some way, and for lack of other ideas, she was content to listen.

Ondechiara.

Even the name was somehow magical. She'd read it on the bottom of the picture enough times to know it by heart. "What does it mean?" She'd asked Michael, on one of the first occasions she'd gone to his flat and seen the picture.

"Clear waves. It's perfect." His smile had been like sunshine. Back then, he'd smiled at her often. She'd come to fear his smile though, because she knew it was a brief burst of warmth, almost always followed by a deafening thunderstorm. "The city itself is quite ancient. Cobbled streets that wind through tiny stone buildings, all brightly coloured and washed by the sea. The roofs are terracotta and the smell of citrus is everywhere. The ocean is the most striking shade of green, but as it comes into shore, the waves become clear, like glass, so you can see every grain of sand on the ocean floor."

"Do you go there often?"

"I've only been once." He lifted his broad shoulders, his body strong, his frame bulky. "With one of my closest friends."

"Well, I think it sounds perfect. I'd love to see it."

"I'll take you there one day."

Michael was good at making promises, but he was much better at breaking them.

She lifted a hand to her throat unconsciously, wincing as she felt the sore flesh there, concealed beneath her turtleneck. After the last time, he'd promised he'd never touch her again. He'd promised he was sorry, that he hadn't meant it, that he'd get help. He'd promised he'd stop gambling, drinking. That he would do anything rather than lose her.

But two weeks later, he'd pinned her to the fridge and gripped her around the neck until she'd truly thought she might die.

Michael had broken every promise that mattered to her.

She paid cash for her ticket to Rome, despite the fact he didn't have access to her bank statements. She couldn't afford to let her guard down. She needed to get away first, to think, to work out what she'd do next.

Ondechiara wouldn't shelter her forever, but perhaps with a little time she'd be able to see the grains of sand that made up her fractured, confusing life a little more clearly. Perhaps she'd be able to float once more...

CHAPTER 1

I F SHE HADN'T BEEN wearing that yellow hat, he'd never have seen her. But from where he stood in the middle of the floor to ceiling windows that made a wall of glass in his home on the edge of the cliff, rain buffeting the glass so that it was grey and almost impossible to see through, he was aware of a slight figure being pushed by the breeze, the rain that was coming in sideways dragging the summery dress around her slender frame.

He didn't think twice. Nico Montebello paced to the front door and wrenched it open, so a gale force wind blew through the architecturally designed home, rattling a painting that hung in the hallway. He strode onto the deck and took the steps two at a time, crossing the grassed cliff top until he was within reach of her.

Her hair was silky blonde, long and fell halfway down her back. It was wet though, clinging to her like seaweed does the water in the ocean. Her tan was golden, proof of a summer spent somewhere like this, and yet he'd never seen her before. *Ondechiara* wasn't a large town, he knew most people in the close-knit community. A *frisson* of caution danced across his spine. This was private land and there'd been a lot of press interest surrounding his family since Fiero and Elodie's wedding. *The first Montebello Bachelor bites the dust*! The papers had cried, speculating on who would be next to settle down. Little did they know the curse of the Montebellos was a hard one to shake. Fiero had been lucky but Nico found it hard to believe his brothers or cousins would enjoy a similar fate, despite what the tabloids might wish.

Si, she could definitely be a reporter, coming to snoop around. It wouldn't be the first time, though new security measures should have made it almost impossible for a trespasser to gain access to this land.

Which meant she must be really good at her job…

His first reaction of concern was muted to one of suspicion. He approached her from behind. She wasn't looking around as a reporter might. Nor was she doing anything to avoid being seen. That damned yellow hat was like a beacon against the grey sky the summer storm had dragged in over the ancient town and usually crystal clear sea that surrounded this part of Italy.

When he was close enough to be heard, he shouted, "*Basta.*" She jumped half a foot off the ground as she turned to face him.

"Oh my God!" Up close, it was impossible not to be struck by her beauty. Wide-set eyes with an almost turquoise colour, long black lashes that were clumpy and thick from the rain, a fine nose with a slight lift at its end, skin that was tanned caramel, lips that were shaped like a cupid's bow, and cheeks that had dimples in them when she smiled, which she was doing now. "This weather is wild."

Another flash of lightning. She was saturated. "What the hell are you doing here?"

She had to shout to be heard above the lashing rain.

"Exploring." An impish grin. Something surged inside of him that he was eminently familiar with. Desire. Curiosity. That first flush of interest he felt when he met a woman he wanted to know better. It was ridiculous, given that she could very well be here to write an expose on his family.

"This is private property."

She lifted a brow. "Really?" Her gaze drifted to the ocean, so churned up by the wind and waves that it looked dramatic and angry. "It should be illegal to privatise views like this."

Curiosity grew. "You're drenched."

Another smile. "I know."

"You shouldn't be out in this weather."

"I didn't mean to be," she turned back to face him and there it was again: desire, a rolling wave seizing his insides, making it difficult to think of anything else. "It was sunny when I set out."

"It's been raining most of the day."

She lifted her shoulders. "I've been exploring most of the day."

She was probably not a journalist but the likelihood of her being a tiny bit crazy was increasing.

Lightning slashed closer, the bright light dancing towards the sand so Nico swore and gestured to the house. Of the six Montebellos, he was perhaps the most notoriously guarded with his privacy, so he was surprised to hear himself say, "You should wait out the storm here."

Her smile dropped. "Oh, no," she shook her head. "I'm fine."

His eyes narrowed. "Where are you staying?"

Her lips tugged downward into a frown that was bordering on a pout. Mentally, Nico swore. She was somehow even more attractive when she was frowning.

"I'm not planning to stalk you," he assured her drily, so she laughed.

"Sorry." But there was something in her expression, a hint of wariness that had him wondering. "I rented *la villetta di pietra* for the summer."

He made a noise of disbelief but the pouring rain devoured it. "That's eight miles away."

"Is it? So far?"

He stared at her. "You walked here?"

She nodded.

"In the rain?"

Another nod.

That settled it. "You can't possibly walk back now."

"The storm should clear soon."

"It won't. It isn't blowing out to sea, it's settling in."

"How do you know?" She looked towards the ocean so he had a glimpse of her elegant, swan-like neck, the skin there smooth and golden.

"I know." He gestured to his house once more. "Come and wait it out."

She looked at him thoughtfully, hesitantly. It was an unusual response. Nico was used to women tripping over themselves to be alone with him, but this woman seemed to be genuinely uncertain.

"It's a simple neighbourly invitation," he heard himself promise. "Nothing sinister whatsoever."

"How do I know that?" Her arched brow held a challenge.

"That I don't have any nefarious intent?"

"Right."

"You don't." His own grin was unknowingly charming. "You'll have to trust me."

"I don't trust easily."

Admiration shifted inside of him; he recognised the trait and appreciated it. He'd trusted easily once and it had burned him. He didn't make a habit of it anymore. "Nor do I."

Her eyes shone like the sea on a sunlit day but when she spoke, the words were swallowed completely by the storm.

"Better to trust me than this weather," he shouted to be heard.

She bit down on her lower lip then jumped as another slash of lightning burst through the sky. A few seconds later, the accompanying rumble of thunder burst overhead and a strong wind threatened to blow the hat right off her head.

"Just until it passes."

"Bene." He nodded approvingly at her common sense, leading the way back to the house. The timber deck was a little slippery so he held a hand out in an offer of support. She ignored it, side-stepping the boots and Dante's leash with grace and ease, pausing just inside the door while she looked around. Her eyes spun through the hall and into the living area, which caused him to do the same, viewing it as she must be. It was unmistakably grand. White marble flooring that gave way to walls of glass framing spectacular views of the ocean in one direction and the countryside in the other. A grand piano sat down the far side of the room, and priceless art adorned the walls.

"Nice place to wait out a storm," she quipped, lifting her hat off and holding it in her hands. Her nails were bare of colour and cut short.

"Grazie." The door blew closed with a fierce bang before he could catch it and she flinched, whipping around to face him as though he'd purposefully made the noise. "Sorry," he lifted his hands, her actions reminding him a little of Dante when he'd first inherited the dog and he'd been wary as a default setting.

"What for?" She covered it so quickly that he wondered if he'd invented her response.

"You're soaking. Let me get you some clothes," he offered.

"Thank you."

He was glad she didn't refuse, because he didn't really want to argue with her, nor did he want her pneumonia on his conscience. He had only his own clothes to offer and there was a substantial size difference between them. He pulled out a sweater and a pair of board shorts that had a drawstring waist, as well as some socks. When he returned to the lounge room, she was staring at one of the paintings – a landscape of the area that had been done by a well-known impressionist. It had been turned into a print at some point, and was sold all over the world.

Her eyes flicked to his. "I'm making a puddle."

"*Di niente.* I have towels."

Her eyes held his in a way that was compelling and unnerving. "This is beautiful."

"*Si.*" He moved towards it. "It captures Ondechiara well."

She nodded. "It's the original?"

"*Si.*"

"Wow." The word escaped her lips so softly he barely heard it.

"Here. There's not much but at least it will keep you warm for now."

"Thanks." She looked around. "Is there somewhere…?"

"Of course," he nodded crisply. "The door on the left." He gestured down the corridor. As she walked towards the powder room, he found his eyes following her without his consent, studying the lithe grace of her step, the gentle curve of her rear, her neat waist. He dragged his gaze away with effort, turning his attention to the water she'd leaked onto the marble floor. Grabbing a towel from the linen press, he'd just finished drying it when she returned.

His desire now was no stealth-like whisper. It was a throb, a drum beating intensely in his gut, pulsing through his body in a way that was unsettling, given the promise he'd rendered in order to convince her to take shelter.

"What are you doing so far from *la viletta?*" His voice was thick, strangled by his throat.

"I told you," she smiled, her wet hands clutched in her hands. "Exploring."

He moved towards her, noting more details up close. She wore no make up – or perhaps she had, but it had all been washed off now. She didn't need cosmetics. She had a beauty that was completely natural, her bone structure so fine, her complexion stunning. She'd towel-dried her hair and pulled it over one shoulder and the size of his sweater meant the fine bones of her décolletage were displayed to him.

"Can these go in the machine?"

She pulled a face that was borderline teasing. "Yeah. You don't need to bother…"

"We're stuck here til the storm passes. It's no trouble."

"If you're sure."

He held a hand out by way of acceptance and she placed the clothes in them. The gesture was unconscious but it brought them nearer; up close, there was a hint of citrus surrounding her, as though she'd been kissed by the grove to the east of the house. Her eyes flared wide, as though she too felt this zip of awareness, this hum of need, and neither of them moved for several seconds. They stared at each other so he caught every detail of her response. Her lips parted and her breath was warm, fanning against his Adam's apple. A hint of colour flared in her cheeks, and the fine pulse point at the base of her throat trembled visibly.

Curiosity strangled him.

"I…" Her voice was soft. She swallowed, as if struggling to grab the threads of her thoughts. "I didn't realise this was a house. I wouldn't have encroached on your privacy…"

"*Di niente.*" He shook his head, and it was like breaking a spell – or postponing its hold at least. "I'll be right back."

But she padded behind him, so that as he pushed the

towels and her clothes into the washer, he was conscious of her leaning against the doorjamb watching him with an undisguised curiosity of her own. "You're more domesticated than you look."

He added a tablet and shut the door, pressed some buttons then stood. "You don't know that – I could very well have ruined your clothes by putting them on the wrong setting."

She shrugged. "That's true."

And though he knew he should resist the temptation to flirt with her, he heard himself say, "And what do I look like…?"

"Maddie," she supplied, perhaps to take an easy way out of answering his question.

"Maddie," he repeated. It suited her. Soft and sweet but somehow confident too. "Well?" He prompted.

"You look like a man who's never used a washing machine in his life," she said after a slight pause. "Or maybe it's just that this place looks like it should come with an army of help…"

He laughed at that. "True. But I prefer to be alone when I'm in Ondechiara."

"You don't live here?"

"No."

"Ah." She nodded. "So you're just renting the place? Like a holiday home?"

He frowned. In the village he was well known, but beyond that, the Montebello name was a global one. That she didn't know who he was a fascinating novelty. "No. It's mine."

She narrowed her gaze speculatively and for a brief second he was reminded of his initial belief that she might be a journalist. "It's beautiful."

"*Si.*" He stepped towards her, intending to leave the

usually light-filled laundry, but she didn't shift, so his movement simply brought them close once more. "And what brings you to this tiny little town on the edge of Italy, Maddie?" He liked saying her name. It rolled off his tongue in a way that was addictive.

For the briefest moment, her smile slipped and her eyes darkened. It was a striking contrast to the easy amusement he'd enjoyed seeing moments earlier. "That's a long story."

He looked over his shoulder, to the rain that was lashing the window behind him, casting the room in gloom. "We seem to have a bit of time."

"True," she murmured, straightening, but still not moving, and not answering his question. Their eyes were locked and though they weren't touching, the look was intimate and unnerving, addictive and heated. She broke the spell this time. "Do you mind if I make a cup of tea?"

"Of course." He was surprised by his lack of manners.

She stepped back now, allowing him to pass, but as he did so, their arms brushed and he felt a burst of awareness, so he tilted his head towards her. She was staring at him, stricken, and he understood. The tension bubbling between them was arcing two ways, a powerful electrical current that was somehow intensified by the storm raging beyond the house.

She followed behind him – he felt her – into the large kitchen that opened off the lounge room. "Have a seat," he gestured to the stools parked at the marble bench top.

"I can make it. I don't want to put you..."

"It's no trouble," he repeated, flicking the kettle on and pulling a mug from the pantry. For himself, he scooped some coffee into the coffee cradle and pressed a button, watching as the dark liquid began to pool into his espresso cup. "You were telling me why you're in Ondechiara?"

"Was I?"

She was intentionally evasive. It sparked curiosity and a

hint of caution – hadn't he learned his lesson about women who were secretive by nature? He didn't want to think of Claudette though. He'd promised himself a long time ago that she didn't deserve his consideration after what she'd done.

"You don't have to if you'd prefer not to discuss it." His words were unintentionally clipped, the ghost of Claudette filling him with reminders of disgust – at her easy deception and his gullibility.

"Thank you."

Her response surprised him. She made no attempt to obfuscate, no attempt to lie. She simply chose not to answer him.

He studied her more thoughtfully now, new possibilities opening up to him. Was she a runaway? A fugitive?

"I'm not a criminal or anything," she promised him, laughing now, the sound bursting into the room relaxing him, pleasing him, mending the tear Claudette had forced between them. "It's just...something I'm still making sense of," she offered. "And I prefer to keep to myself. You know?"

He lifted one brow, her words echoing his own mantra. "I do."

She bit down on her lip so he had to ball his hands at his side to resist the temptation to reach across and smudge his thumb over the soft pink flesh.

"How long have you been here? Or would you prefer not to answer that as well?"

"No," she shook her head, a smile playing about the corners of her lips. "About six months."

Surprise shifted inside of him. "I haven't seen you around."

"No," she lifted her shoulders.

"Because you like to keep to yourself?"

He put a teabag into the cup and poured the water over it.

"I guess so," but she was smiling. "Part of the appeal of the place I rented was that it was secluded. I love that. I feel like I'm right on the edge of the earth." She angled her face towards the window, staring out at the stormy view. "I go into town for supplies, but other than that, I like my own company."

"For six months?"

"Uh huh."

"And you walk."

"Yep."

"Why here?"

"Ondechiara?" Her skin paled perceptibly.

He let it pass. "No. Why here, my villa?"

"Oh." She sipped her tea, her eyes holding his over the edge of the mug. "I remember seeing it the first day I arrived. This big, beautiful building high on the cliffs. I was fascinated by it – the way it seems to be cast from the stone that surrounded it yet totally modern at the same time. It's a beautiful contradiction."

"But you haven't been here before?"

"No," she shook her head. "I felt like a long walk today," she shrugged. "I don't remember even consciously deciding to set out for this place."

"There's security fencing."

"I came up the steps. From the beach."

He swore under his breath. "They're disused for a reason, Maddie. They're incredibly dangerous. Didn't you notice the fallen rocks?"

She flinched – just a small, involuntary movement that had him softening his tone. "There's a locked gate."

"It was an open gate when I got there."

"The wind must have blown it off its hinges." He shook his head, because that shouldn't have been possible and yet the only option was that she'd scaled a six foot construction – which didn't seem likely.

"I didn't notice," she admitted, a hint of guilt crossing her face.

"I'll have it fixed."

"So how do you get down to the beach?"

"I drive."

"But you're right here, above it. Why don't you get the stairs fixed?"

He frowned. "I would, if I used the beach." He took a drink of his espresso. "By the way, that whole stretch of the beach is private too. There were definitely signs, right? Or had they also been blown away?"

A hint of blush spread through her cheeks. "No, there were signs saying 'private property'. I presumed they were planted in error. I mean, beaches shouldn't be private, right?"

He laughed. "Why do I get the feeling you're trouble, Maddie?"

"Because I don't like to listen to bossy signs?"

He made a growling noise of assent.

"I truly presumed this was an art gallery or something."

"An art gallery that was only accessible by perilous steps from the beach?"

"No. Naturally I thought there was a street somewhere too."

"There is."

"Let me guess, it's gated though."

"*Si*." He shrugged his broad shoulders, noting the way her eyes dropped to the gesture, following the outline of his body. "I like to keep to myself too."

"I'm sorry to have intruded," she lifted her gaze to his face and he felt the same flash of electricity firing deep in his gut.

Pleasure and anticipation stirred inside of him, even as he knew he should fight it. She was staring at him with those enormous blue eyes and his body was responding even as his mind was trying to retain control. She was staring at him and slowly he shook his head, and when he spoke there was a gruff resignation in his voice, as though he knew there was a game of fate afoot, one that would get the better of him.

"I'm not."

CHAPTER 2

B REATHE. JUST, BREATHE. Maddie wrapped her
hands around the mug and tried not to stare at him.
But she was fighting a losing battle because he was *beyond*
addictive and she found her eyes inhaling him at every
opportunity.

She'd never really gone for the 'tall, dark and handsome'
guys, or so she'd thought, but this specimen of masculinity
was breath-takingly intoxicating. He was easily six and a half
feet tall and his build was slim, but at the same time, muscular, his skin a deep tan, his hair brown with a hint of gold at
the front from where he'd spent time in the sun. But it was
his eyes that had her fixated. They were a spectacular blue,
flicked with gold, and the lashes surrounding them were
thick and dark. His jaw was squared, but covered in the hint
of stubble that made her fingertips itch with a desire to lift
up and touch.

What the heck was happening to her?

She'd been stupid to keep walking when it had started to
pour with rain, but it had been light enough and she'd
presumed it would pass. Then, she'd got a little lost and

before she'd known it she was on the beach beneath the enormous construction she'd been wondering about since she'd come to Ondechiara.

"You're warm enough?"

"I'm fine, thanks," she nodded, forcing herself to hold his eyes even when the intensity of his stare spread wildfire through her veins. "So what do you do when you're not rescuing stray tourists from cliff tops?"

The briefest hint of a frown crossed his face. "I'm in finance." The words were a little uneasy. She wondered if there was a problem with his job. The global finance industry had been in turmoil lately, it was possible he'd been caught up in that. She didn't want to pry, particularly if he'd recently been made redundant or similar.

She was lucky to be immune from that kind of considera-tion in her line of work. "I've always admired people who are good with numbers," she said, instead. "I've never had much of a head for them."

"Everyone has a head for numbers."

She pulled a face. "I beg to differ."

"Maths is everywhere," he pointed out, finishing his coffee and placing it in the sink.

"And I use it as little as possible."

"It's hard to avoid."

"I've made it an art form," she winked, and wished she hadn't when he formed a slow, sensual grin in response.

"What do you do then? When you're not avoiding numbers like the plague."

She sipped her tea. "I'm a writer."

For the briefest moment, something shifted in his expres-sion, so he was stern and alert. "As in a journalist?"

She shook her head. "No. As in a fiction writer. A novelist."

"Seriously?"

She nodded.

"Would I have read anything you've written?"

She bit down on her lip. "I doubt it. I sell okay in the UK and Australia, but not anywhere else yet." She lifted her shoulders. "It's a labour of love, but at least the hours are flexible and I can do it from anywhere in the world."

"So you're here for research?" He prompted after a moment.

A smile lifted the corner of her lips. "Yeah, I guess you could say that. It's kind of a writer's retreat," she substituted. "I needed a break. From home." She sipped her tea quickly, choking on it a little.

"Where's home?"

"England." It was a vague answer that told him nothing he didn't presumably already know, given her accent. She couldn't help it. In the six months since leaving London, she'd received several text messages from Michael each week. It was impossible to feel safe and as though she was out of the woods when he was still reaching out to her. Every time she saw his name on her phone, she panicked. It was like being dragged back into their home, back into his life, the sensation suffocating and cloying.

"London?"

She stood up a little jerkily and moved towards the large windows. "You were right about the storm. It's not showing any sign of letting up."

He was quiet for a few moments and she held her breath, wondering if he was going to let her conversation change go. But after a few moments, his voice came from right behind her. "Our summer storms tend to be like that. There aren't many, but when they come, they're violent as all hell." She lifted her gaze to his face, marvelling at the strength there, a bone structure that reminded her a little of the cliff face she'd scaled earlier that day. "When I was a boy, I was here with my grandfather and Yaya when a storm came through. It destroyed half the town, including this place."

She looked around, taking in the grandness of the house with fresh eyes. As if reading her thoughts, he murmured, "Oh, it didn't used to look like this."

"No?"

"It was far more rustic." He lifted a hand, running it over the smooth, white wall. "My grandfather grew up here. His parents didn't have much money and the house was basic. But beautiful. Big open rooms coming off a central hallway, terracotta roof, lime-washed walls, and the smell of salt and sand and fish everywhere. The walls were the strangest colour – like sand, I suppose – yellow brown, but I can't see that colour without feeling a yearning for this place."

Her smile was instinctive. "It sounds a lot like La Villetta."

"I've never been inside," he murmured, his voice like melted chocolate. "But *certamente,* the exteriors would indicate they were constructed around the same time."

"The first time I saw La Villetta, I felt like I'd stepped into a postcard of Italy. It was everything I'd imagined."

"You hadn't been here before?"

"To Ondechiara? Never."

"To Italy, though?"

"To Rome and Venice."

His lips showed a hint of derision. "The tourist hotspots."

"Guilty as charged," she responded in kind, earning a grin from him that seared something in the pit of her stomach. "I was blown away by the beauty of this place. The village is lovely, of course, and the people friendly, but it's the countryside I'm besotted with. Rolling hills in a dozen different shades of green, roads that carve their way across the hills' undulations, flowers that seem to burst with life, fruit that fills the air with the most divine fragrance." She shook her head a little. "And there, in the middle of nowhere, on the edge of a little tributary, is La Villetta di Pietra, all stone-washed walls and tiled floors, a garden with geraniums and lavender, and goats just across the field." She wasn't aware of the way his eyes dropped to her smile, studying her in a way that would have made her heart flip and flop if she'd noticed it.

"It's like something out of a fairy tale. I feel so safe here."

"Safe?" He prompted and inwardly, she admonished herself for employing such a telling word.

"You know, calm. It's nice." The response was awkward. She lifted her face to his and finally saw the way he was looking at her, so her breath snagged in her throat and she felt an odd rush of feeling. Of many feelings, all tangled together so she couldn't understand how she was feeling, nor why. There was guilt, certainly, because her body was warm all over, her pulse throbbing, her heart racing, her fingertips aching with a need to reach out and touch this man. Why should she feel guilty, though? Because of Michael? The very idea sparked defiance in her chest. He'd already taken enough from her. He'd hurt her enough. He didn't get to have any place in this – he was a completely separate part of her life.

That was why she was here, in Italy. Because here she could start fresh. No one knew what she'd been through. His eyes dropped to her lips and her heart lurched because she wanted, more than anything, to feel his lips on hers. A tiny sound escaped her lips – something between a groan and a plea – but it was enough to startle her. She took a small step back, smiled tightly and returned her attention to the view.

"And you like calm?"

His own voice was gravelled and it sparked a tsunami of need in her belly. She tamped down on it with effort.

"Who doesn't?"

He was quiet and despite her best intentions, she found her eyes lifting to his.

"Why do you come here?"

Surprise flashed in his eyes. "The same reasons as you, I suspect."

Maddie doubted that, but she didn't say as much. To deny his assertion was to invite questions she wasn't willing to answer. She hadn't spoken to anyone about Michael. She couldn't, and it was so hard to explain why. She hated that she felt a degree of shame for what had happened to her, because she understood it was completely out of her control, but it was hard to admit to what had happened – no, it was hard to admit why she'd stayed after the first time he'd hit her. She'd truly believed though that he'd made a mistake. It had seemed so out of character at the time, except it wasn't, obviously.

She'd left London, telling her parents she had a deadline and needed to write away from distraction, telling her friends only that she and Michael had broken up without fleshing out any further details. And she told no one where she was going. She didn't dare risk it. Michael was charming and clever and could undoubtedly persuade someone to open up to him about her location.

It had been instinctive to keep her secrets close to her chest but now, in the presence of a man she'd known for less than an hour, she felt a compelling desire to speak truthfully. Perhaps it was the anonymity that came of spending time with someone you didn't know, and likely wouldn't see again?

Or perhaps it was more complicated than that, she admitted grudgingly, as she flicked her gaze to his face once more. He was a stranger to her and yet she felt an instinctive tug towards him, a trust she wanted to be guided by even when she knew better than to rely on her instincts. Instincts that had, after all, guided her to Michael.

"I don't even know your name," she said with a small shake of her head, the intensity of this overwhelming.

"It's Nico," he provided, his eyes scanning her features, as if looking for something – she couldn't say what.

"Nico." She repeated it, smiling, because it was perfect for him. "Is it short for anything?"

"Niccolo," he nodded. "Conqueror of the people," his voice assumed a deeper tone and he posed his features into a mask of strength so she laughed.

"Perfect."

"*Si?*"

The question surprised her, because it forced her to admit that yes, she'd been speaking honestly. There was something about him that spoke of victory and conquering, of being conquered.

How she wished she had a tighter grip on her body's responses! But she didn't – a force was at work that was so much bigger than her. Desire was flaring in the pit of her stomach and even when she could think of a dozen reasons to ignore it, she knew she absolutely didn't want to.

"Yeah." She angled her body to face his, her pulse racing, her tempo firing. Was she really going to do this? Do what? Her brain screamed. He might not be interested in her. She might be misreading everything. Before Michael, it had been a really long time before she'd dated anyone. She wasn't good at this stuff.

And he was really gorgeous. Undoubtedly he could have his pick of anyone. Lightning flashed just beyond the window and she startled. It wasn't much. Just an involuntary shiver – barely enough to register. But his hand shot out, as if to steady her, his strong fingers curving around her arm. The lightest touch, so gentle and reassuring, but it shot little arrows of awareness through her bloodstream and made her cheeks burn with heat.

"You're okay?" He murmured. Had he moved closer? Or had she? They stood toe to toe, so she had to crane her neck to meet his eyes now. She could feel his chest moving with each breath he drew.

She nodded, sucking in a gulp of air that was peppered with his intoxicatingly masculine fragrance.

"Yeah, I'm fine."

"You're jumpy."

She was. She had been since Michael. Her lips twisted into a grimace. "Yeah. Sometimes."

"You don't need to be." A divot formed between his brows. "You're safe here."

Had he intentionally chosen the word she'd let slip earlier? She bit down on her lower lip, chewing it distractedly. "Am I?"

A growling noise of agreement. She lifted her hand and pressed it to his chest, surprising them both. "I don't know if I want to feel safe right now."

He closed his eyes for a moment, his face unreadable. "No?"

Her blood was rushing so fast she could hear it in her ears. She shook her head slowly, her eyes holding his in a courageous display of need. "Nope."

"Maddie," her name on his lips was a sensual incantation, but he stayed where he was. "I didn't invite you here for this."

Insecurities cut through her desire. She dropped her hand and spun away from him. "Oh, God. I know. I'm sorry. I don't know what came over me." She shook her head, unable to look at him, staring across the room. "You've been really kind and I shouldn't…"

His fingers curved around her wrist, pulling at her gently. "The same thing that came over you has come over me too," he promised and her heart skipped a beat. "But I invited you to shelter here with no agenda. I need to know you believe that, that you won't think I'm taking advantage of the situation."

Pleasure flooded her heart. So considerate. So kind. But Michael had seemed like that at the start, too. He'd seemed so perfect. She bit down on her lip, swallowing the bitterness that cloyed at her throat.

Nico wasn't Michael, and nor was she the same woman she'd been then. And she wasn't looking for a relationship – she'd learned her lesson there. God knew if she'd ever feel secure enough to want to pursue anything long term. But in this moment, with this man, she wanted enough to cloud her doubts and questions. The future felt a long way away, tomorrow in another universe.

"And if I want to take advantage of the situation?" She murmured, lifting up onto the tips of her toes so their lips were just an inch apart.

"*Dio aiutami,*" he groaned.

"What does that mean?"

"It means God help me," he muttered, but the last words were smothered by his lips as he crushed them to hers. It was a kiss of complete and total possession. Her knees felt weak and his arm clamped behind her back as though he knew without his support she might slide right to the ground.

Stars exploded through her mind, celestial dust blowing through all her dark spaces, filling her with light and heat and warmth. His other hand cradled her head, his fingers pushing through her damp hair so she moaned, opening her mouth wider. Their tongues duelled but it wasn't a fight; no, it was a capitulation in every sense of the world. Only she didn't feel as though she was surrendering; she felt victorious, as though she was reclaiming an important part of herself. As though this simple act of passion could stitch something of Madeleine Gray back into place, just as she'd been before Michael.

Her hands, pressed to his chest, sought his shirt, pushing it so her fingertips could connect with the naked expanse of his muscular abdomen. He was so warm. He said something in his native tongue, the word firing through her body, landing in the pit of her abdomen. Need grew. The storm raged wild outside their window but neither heard it – their own storm was so much more intense, so much more demanding. He lifted her easily, holding her body pressed to his own as he carried her through the house, shouldering a door to a darkened room.

"Presumptuous?" He asked with a sexy grin as he flicked a light switch on. She looked around for just long enough to ascertain that they were in a bedroom.

"Nope." Her hands found his shirt again and now she pushed it up his body. "Perfect."

"The bedroom or my body?" He teased.

"Both." But she was kissing him again, her hands working the button of his pants, unfastening them so she could shove them down his legs without breaking their kiss. He stepped out of them with the same degree of urgency and she laughed – for no reason except that she was deliriously happy.

He wore only his boxers. And at that point, she slowed, uncertainty rocking her. Doubts plagued her. It had been a long time since she'd done this. And he was so different. *So* different to anyone she'd ever known.

"You are so beautiful," he muttered darkly and the words brought her right back to the present, dragging her into the room, filling her with sensual awareness. There was no room for doubt. This was right. It was perfect, just like she'd said.

She lifted her hands into the air, her eyes holding an unspoken invitation. Everything about him was remarkable.

She saw the way his throat shifted, his Adam's apple bobbing as he swallowed, and then he was lifting the jumper he'd given her, pulling it softly over her head and dropping it to the floor.

She should have felt more self-conscious but she didn't. Even when his eyes dropped, so he was staring at her, taking in every detail, and her nipples pulled taut and began to feel tingly.

"So beautiful." The words were deep, but his smile was sexy and sweet all at once. He shook his head, almost as though he couldn't believe it, and she wanted to tell him such extravagant praise wasn't necessary – she didn't need it and it was hard to believe it was true. She hated that too though – Michael had made it so easy to discredit any compliment anyone paid her. *He's just saying it because he wants to get into your pants,* Michael would have pointed out – quite rightly.

Just like he had when her editor had praised her latest book. *It's a true work of art, Madeleine.* Michael had naturally laughed. *Well, they've already bought it, right? A bit late to tell you it's meaningless crap given your copy editing deadline.*

"No words," she said, lifting a finger and pressing it to his lips. "It's easier."

He pulled a face. "Really?"

"Uh huh."

"As easy as this?" He grabbed her by the hips and lifted her, dropping her unceremoniously onto the bed so she laughed as she scrambled onto her elbows.

"As easy as what?"

"This." He wrapped his mouth around one of her nipples, his tongue circling the sensitive flesh, teasing it, rolling it, pulling it so she whimpered and arched her back, desire driving her utterly wild. Heat pooled between her legs.

"God," she cried and felt him smile against her breast. His finger and thumb pressed to her other nipple, clamping down on it with just enough pressure to make stars shoot against her eyelids. "This is…God."

"I thought we weren't talking?" He mocked, bringing the full weight of his body down over her, his arousal between her legs a stark reminder of what was about to happen. A kaleidoscope of butterflies rampaged her belly.

"I meant…compliments…" she groaned as he rolled his hips, pressing his arousal to her sex so despite the barrier of his boxers and the shorts he'd given her, she was incandescent with pleasure.

"I can't tell you you're beautiful?"

"You don't need to tell me," she corrected, pushing at his boxers, needing more, needing to feel him, needing to be possessed by him. "Please," she whimpered into the room.

He pulled up, shifting his mouth to her other nipple but this time, instead of closing his mouth over it, he simply flicked it with his tongue. It was already so sensitive from the way his finger and thumb had been toying with it seconds ago, so the sheer hint of contact from his mouth sent her senses into overdrive. His hands roamed her body, running down her sides with a lightness of touch that was infuriating because it was simply not enough. She needed everything he could give her and she needed it immediately.

At her waist, his hands found the elastic of her shorts and pushed them down, easing them from her body. She lifted her bottom off the mattress to make it easier.

His hands didn't leave her legs long, once he'd discarded the shorts. Starting at her ankles, they began a slow cruise upwards, towards her thighs, where he pushed a little, separating her legs. She groaned, writhing on the bed beneath him, impatient, hungry for him.

"Don't forget a condom," she was shocked she'd managed to remember.

"I will. When it's time."

She didn't get a chance to ask what he meant. His mouth connected with her sex, his tongue, his clever, clever tongue moving slowly at first, and then more intently, buzzing her sensitive cluster of nerves until she was burning up. It was so intimate her cheeks flamed, but she didn't think, for even one moment, of asking him to stop. Instead, her hands found his hair, running through it, holding on as pleasure threatened to burst through her, tearing her apart completely.

When she was at the brink of breaking, he moved faster, his tongue tormenting her, lashing her until she was trembling. She arched her back and pushed down against him and then she was tumbling off the edge of the earth, exploding against his mouth, exploding with his name on her lips over and over again.

It was unrelenting. Even as she came, he didn't stop, so she was fire and flame, desperate for him even as she was at the end of her tolerance for pleasure. He somehow knew – he understood, and pulled away, moving his mouth to her inner thigh, kissing the flesh there before moving back to her sex, kissing her more gently, allowing her time to breathe, to recover before he began his next incursion. This time, a finger moved inside of her and she moaned, shaking her head, desperate and terrified of the strength of her desperation even as she knew she would happily surrender to this anytime, anywhere.

He watched her in a way that made her feel precious and special and sexier than sin. He watched her in a way that she loved, like he wanted to understand everything about her so he could pleasure her over and over. The promise was delicious but she pushed it away. This wasn't about promises. It was just this. Sex. No, not just sex. It was more. It was a healing, a balm, an undoing of Michael, overwriting the memories of how he'd treated her body with this: someone who was worshipping her, existing purely to pleasure her.

It was a physical act with an emotional resonance that she didn't want to analyse in that moment.

And it was only just beginning.

JUST THIS ONE SUMMER is available in October 2019 but you can pre-order the book for the special pre-release price of 99c until that date.

BOOKS BY CLARE CONNELLY

HARLEQUIN TITLES

Bought for the Billionaire's Revenge

Innocent in the Billionaire's Bed

Off Limits

Her Wedding Night Surrender

Burn Me Once

Bound by the Billionaire's Vows

The Season to Sin

His Innocent Seduction

Bound by their Christmas Baby

Her Guilty Secret

Shock Heir for the King

The Greek's Billion-Dollar Baby

Spaniard's Baby of Revenge

The Bride Behind the Billion-Dollar Veil

The Deal

Cross my Hart (Notorious Harts Bk 1)

SINGLE TITLES

Regret Me Not

Just This One Summer

Loving The Enemy

Her Guardian's Christmas Seduction

Stolen by the Desert King

In the Hands of the Sheikh

His Nine Month Seduction

The Sheikh's Contract Bride

Seduced by the Vengeful Tycoon

The Sheikh's Stolen Bride

The Sheikh's Secret Baby

The Sheikh's Million Dollar Bride

The Tycoon's Virgin Mistress

The Sheikh's Virgin Hostage

Bartered to the Sheikh

The Sheikh's Arranged Marriage

Marrying for his Royal Heir

The Greek's Marriage Revenge

The Velasco Love Child

The Sultan's Virgin Bride

Bound to the Sheikh

The Medici Mistress

His Loving Deception

The Sheikh's Convenient Mistress

The Princess's Forbidden Lover

Marrying her Enemy

Rakanti's Indecent Proposition

Seducing the Spaniard

The Italian's Innocent Bride

The Greek Tycoon's Forbidden Affair

The Terms of their Affair

A Second Chance at Love

The Sheikh's Christmas Mistress

At the Sheikh's Command

The Billionaire's Christmas Revenge

Seduced by the Italian Tycoon

Raising the Soldier's Son

Warming the Sheikh's Bed

The Tycoon's Christmas Captive

The Brazilian's Forgotten Lover

Betrayed by the CEO

The Billionaire's Ruthless Revenge

The Italian Billionaire's Betrayal

The Sultan's Reluctant Princess

Love in the Fast Lane

Bought by the Sheikh

The Tycoon's Summer Seduction

All She Wants for Christmas

One Night with the Sheikh

A Bed of Broken Promises

Tempted by the Billionaire

The Sheikh's Christmas Wish

To the Highest Bidder

The Tycoon's Secret Baby

Bedding His Innocent Mistress

The Sheikh's Baby Bargain

The Greek's Virgin Captive

The Sheikh's Inherited Bride

Claiming His Secret Baby

Blackmailed by the Spaniard

Her Surprise Baby Christmas

COMPENDIUMS

Casacelli Brides

Mediterranean Tycoons

Desert Rulers

Billionaire Bad Boys

Too Hot to Handle

Desert Kings

Happily Ever After

The Darling Buds of May Café

Royal Weddings

The Evermore Series

Made in the USA
Columbia, SC
11 January 2020

86692584R00152